The Last Witch of Scotland

Vidhipssa Mohan

Published by The Pink Hearts, 2020.

This is a work of fiction. Similarities to real people, places, or events are entirely coincidental.

THE LAST WITCH OF SCOTLAND

First edition. August 20, 2020.

Copyright © 2020 Vidhipssa Mohan.

Written by Vidhipssa Mohan.

Dedicated to all the misunderstood witches,

Chapter 1

"Do you believe in witches?" The interviewer who asks me this question looks into my eyes as if he is trying to look within my soul. He is a plain-looking man, the kind of man whose face I'd forget as soon as I step outside the building. I am already nervous, but this question makes me shift in my seat.

"I believe in witches, but not the kind that hex you." I wanted to give a balanced answer, neither too positive nor too negative. Henry doesn't seem satisfied. He looks down at his laptop screen and makes a note. The click-click-click sound of the keyboard echo throughout the silent room. He pauses, looks up at me and gives me a small smile.

"Please elaborate," he says while fixing his glasses and continuing to stare at me as if I am on a witch trial. I feel thirsty and would love a glass of water right now. I haven't drunk any water since morning because I didn't want to keep going to the toilet right before my interview. I look at Henry and I can tell that he knows I am nervous. There is a glass of water on the table but I am not sure if I should drink it right now or if I should answer his question first.

"Would you like a glass of water?" he offers.

"Yes, please." Henry may look plain but he looks like the kind of person who is very intuitive. I can tell that he is good at reading people.

I clear my throat. "We live in a sexist world. Any woman who doesn't conform to the rules of society is called a witch. So clearly, witches that hex you don't exist." I pause and take a sip of my water. "But all women possess magic. They have endured patriarchy for thousands of years and somehow haven't killed the entire species of men." This makes Henry chuckle. I laugh with him too. Perhaps I am too much of a feminist with my answer, but Henry doesn't seem to mind.

"You're right. So, tell me. What made you apply for this job?"

I plaster a smile on my face and lie, "When I read the job description, I felt this job is made for me. I have always been interested in the supernatural, I already spend hours reading about the occult and things that don't seem ordinary. Being paid for something that I already do would be a dream come true for me."

He nods again, I can tell that he is impressed. "Alright, do you know much about witches in Scotland? You're not Scottish, right?" I can't quite place Henry's accent. It's definitely not any of the Scottish accents I've heard. It's the kind of accent you have when you grow up in many places. Like mine.

"No, I was born to Indian parents in England. But I have always been interested in anything and everything Scottish. The culture is so rich. As for your question, I do know a little bit about Scottish witches. Janet Douglas, Lady Glamis, Janet Horne and more. I have read about them. All of them are very interesting figures." The truth is, I don't know anything about Scottish witches. Before coming to this interview, I did a quick Google search and whatever I told Henry was what I found on the first page of Google. I don't even believe in anything magical. I am a very practical person when it comes to life. I believe in facts and figures and nothing else.

Henry is convinced by my lie though. "Wow, you really seem enthusiastic about this. Do you have any experience with research? Your resume tells me you have done your undergraduate degree in International Relations. Won't this job be a completely new direction for you?"

I knew he'd bring this up and I already have an answer prepared. "I think doing my degree made me completely sure that my true passion lies in doing historical research. I didn't enjoy my classes at all and I spent all my time in the library archives reading about witches through the centuries. If I wanted a job in International Relations, I wouldn't have moved to Glasgow for that. I would have simply stayed in Birmingham or moved to London, perhaps."

"Oh, yeah. You recently moved to Glasgow, right?"

"Just last week."

"Oh, so you're still new to the city. It's beautiful here, I am sure you'd enjoy living here."

"I hope so. If I get a good job, I'd be completely relieved." I smile flirtatiously at Henry. Do I find him attractive? Absolutely not. He looks like a complete nerd but if I have to flirt my way to get this job, I'd do it. I am quite desperate for a job, not this job, any job. I need money. I don't have a lot of savings, which is something I should have thought about before moving here. But I just wanted to leave my home as soon as possible.

"Kali, I think it would be fun to work with you on this project," Henry says while still typing away on his keyboard.

"Does that mean I am hired?" My voice sounds high-pitched. I didn't want to seem too desperate but it looks like I've failed.

"Uh, we still have a few more candidates that I need to interview. But you'll hear from me soon, whether you get the job or not."

I nod, shake hands with Henry and leave. I am hopeful I'll get the job, my interview went well and I am well-qualified or at least I made it seem that way.

It's raining outside so I have to run to the nearest subway station. I didn't bring an umbrella with me because I didn't want to carry a big bag with me nor did I bring a jacket that would actually protect me from the rain because I wanted to look presentable.

Once I am inside, I finally breathe. I had planned to go and shop for some formal clothes today after the interview in case I actually get the job but I don't want to do it anymore. It's raining harshly and I've been up since 5 a.m. because I was too nervous for the interview. I am hungry and thirsty and need my bed right now. Shopping can wait.

The train is empty save for a few drunk teenagers on the other side of the carriage. I sit as far away from them as possible and take a deep breath. This was my fourth job interview this week. I lied to Henry; I didn't move to Glasgow last week. I moved here a month ago, and I have been looking for a job ever since. I must have applied for a hundred jobs but no one seems to want me. I don't understand why since I have an alright resume and I am a university graduate. Sure, there must be jobs for me. I am intelligent. Well, I am not completely stupid. There's got to be a job for me out there.

Over the past month, I have interviewed for jobs at publishing houses, newspapers, banks, museums and so many other places. None of them offered me a job. In the beginning, I was honest. If there was something I didn't know how to do or wasn't interested in, I admitted it. I told the truth that I didn't know what they wanted me to do but I'd learn. I am a fast learner. I learnt how to ride a bike in three days. I learnt how to use Photoshop in two hours. But the interviewers didn't seem to appreciate the honesty.

Finding a job shouldn't be this hard. I even went on Facebook forums to find some jobs and only got rude comments. One of them said, "Welcome to the real world, darling." And it does feel like I am in the real world.

This is why everything I told Henry in the interview today was a lie.

I don't even know what exactly being a research assistant would mean. I assume it means I'd have to read a few essays and write a research paper or something like that. I have written papers before during my undergrad; I am sure I'll be fine. As long as I have money and I can pay my bills without surviving, I'll be fine. I don't know what would happen if I don't get the job. I don't want to think about it because then I know I'll have a panic attack while being on this train and I don't think the drunk teenagers would call someone for help.

When I get off the train half an hour later, the rain has stopped, and the sky is clear again.

Glasgow is a beautiful city, although many won't agree with me on that. There are so many things happening here every day. Just last week there was a Beyonce concert in SECC, there are several theatres here, all of them showing new shows every week. There are museums, pubs, shopping centres and so many things. It's hard to be bored in the city... if you have money. I have craved going to concerts and shopping for new things for myself and trying out new restaurants but I have to wait until I get a job.

While Glasgow offers so many things, the area that I live in has nothing. It's a residential area and when you type the name on Google, the top news reports in the area are about suspicious murders and drug dealers. Several people have told me it's not a safe area, but no one has killed me yet. I walk with my keys in my hand whenever I go out, just in case. Today, just like other days, I come outside the subway station and walk to my flat as fast as I can. Once I am inside my building, I am relaxed again.

When I moved here, I booked an Airbnb, but it was getting expensive. I browsed through a few flats online and found a girl who was subletting hers as she was spending the next six months in Berlin for an internship. I took the flat without thinking much. Yes, I can't go outside my flat without thinking about being murdered but at least I have a place to live that isn't burning a hole in my wallet. It's half the price of what I'd pay for rent in London and twice the size. I don't have to share my flat with anyone, which is something that I enjoy very much after living my whole life with other people.

I live alone in this two-bedroom flat. The flat isn't too great, but it has all the basic amenities. It does smell a bit weird sometimes and I have loud neighbours. But I am trying to look at the bright side. Besides, the girl left all her furniture and things behind which I am free to use. I've got a great deal, that's for sure.

I take a long shower and slip into my pyjamas once I am home. That's all I have been wearing since I moved here. I don't have any friends that I can go out with every day nor do I have anywhere to be. I have a set of formal clothes for my interviews and that's about it. I promise myself that once I get a good job and get paid, I am going to treat myself to a shopping spree.

After living my whole life in Birmingham, I wanted a change of scenery. Having been to the Scottish Highlands several times, I knew moving to Scotland was going to be the right decision. So, I impulsively left everything and moved here. Sometimes I wonder if I have made a mistake since I had everything in Birmingham. Friends, a job at a restaurant, a boy I was casually dating but then I think about my mother and I am more than happy that I left. I can make friends again, I can get a new job, I can download Tinder and find someone to sleep with but I needed to leave my mother as soon as I could.

I started applying for jobs even before I moved here but didn't even hear back from any of the places. When I saw an advertisement on the University of Glasgow careers website, I knew I needed to apply. The title of the job was intriguing enough to get me interested. "Looking for Research Assistants to study the lives of witches of Scotland." Who wouldn't be interested? I am a practical person but found the job title interesting regardless. I applied even before reading the description, I was that desperate. The pay is more than I'd need to enjoy my life and money's all that matters at the end of the day.

After my shower, I go to the kitchen to make myself some dinner. I have a few pieces of bread, some cheese and old pizza sauce. Once I get my salary, I am going to treat myself to a lavish dinner too. But for tonight, it's just slices of bread.

I take my bread and go to my bedroom. Back home, my mother had very strict rules about what I could or couldn't do. Eating in my bedroom was one of the things that made my mother furious. But now that I live alone, I can do whatever I want.

I put on an old American sitcom on Netflix. It's been my routine since I have moved here, bingeing Netflix TV shows. If I don't get a job soon, I might finish watching the entire catalogue of Netflix.

I am just done with the first episode when the light in my room flickers and then everything goes dark. Power cuts, ugh. This is the third time since I have moved here that something like this has happened. I look outside the window and I am glad to see I am not the only one sitting in the darkness. Thankfully, my room has a large window, and the moonlight makes it possible for me to not be in complete darkness.

I have to say that Glasgow in darkness looks haunting. There is an old church right outside my flat, a church that was built in the sixth century that gives me creepy vibes. This is the part that I hate about being alone. It's easy to scare myself. The other day there was a spider in my bathroom and I couldn't call anyone to kill it. Eventually, I poured a lot of water on the spider and it drowned.

I switch on the torchlight on my phone and eat my remaining slices of bread in silence. Even my room is starting to cool now that the heater is switched off. I don't like this, I don't like this at all. I sit in the darkness having nothing else to do except scroll through my phone and wait for the lights to come back. I am trying to distract myself from my thoughts. Every time I am in the darkness, I find myself remembering something that happened when I was thirteen.

It was a summer night, and I didn't have to go to school every day. I was sleeping in my bedroom when I felt something jumping on my bed and lying next to me. I was aware of what was happening but it felt like my body was paralysed. I wanted to turn around, I wanted to see who or what it was but I just couldn't move. I screamed and my parents ran up to me. They told me it was only a bad dream since I could move again. And they were right.

Something similar happened again a few years later, this time I was attacked by someone lying next to me in my bed. But once again, when I woke up, there was no one around me. I didn't even call my parents this time. These kinds of incidents happened over and over again. I was traumatised to such an extent that just the thought of sleeping alone at night used to terrify me.

One day my mother took me to a priest to find out what was happening to me and he said that I had the ability to communicate with the supernatural. This made me feel even worse because I didn't want to talk to ghosts at all. When my father found out, he took me to a doctor who told us that I was suffering from sleep paralysis. This was perhaps triggered by my parents' constant fights with each other.

Of course, my parents were never going to get me properly treated. They don't believe in mental illnesses. Because then they'd actually become good parents.

My father got me a puppy when I had my tenth incident of sleep paralysis. Sleeping next to an animal was comforting. I still had those episodes of sleep paralysis but with Ruby next to me, I wasn't much scared. She was rescued from a shelter and was too traumatised to do much. But she soon grew to love me and with her love, I could sleep peacefully at night.

I haven't had those sleep paralysis incidents in a while and I am assuming it's because my anxiety is a lot better now that I have moved away from home. I don't know what I'll do if the power doesn't come back on before I sleep, I probably won't sleep tonight then. I wish Ruby was here.

I am swiping through guys on Tinder when the power comes back on again, and I am relieved. I go to my kitchen to wash my dishes and I see it's raining outside again. In my kitchen, I can hear my neighbours talking and laughing. Most of my neighbours are students, they are always celebrating something and it just makes me feel even lonelier. I'd like to celebrate something too.

It makes me miss my own university days. Perhaps I should get a pet. I can't have a dog because I won't be able to leave him alone.

Perhaps a fish but then I can't cuddle with a fish at night. Maybe a cat but I don't know anything about keeping cats.

When I come back to my laptop after washing my dishes, there is an unread email in my inbox.

"Dear Kali,

Congratulations on your offer from the History Department at the University of Glasgow. We are delighted to offer you the position of Research Assistant with an anticipated start date of September 10th.

As discussed during your interview, please find attached your detailed offer letter. If you choose to accept this offer, please sign, scan, and email your letter to me by 1st September.

In the meantime, please don't hesitate to reach out to me, either through email or by calling me directly if you should have any questions or concerns.

We are looking forward to hearing from you and hope you'll join our team!

Best regards,

Henry Cunningham"

I reread the email twice. Did I get the job? I got the job! I breathe a sigh of relief and now I can finally relax. I keep rereading the email in disbelief thinking if what I have read is actually true and I am not hallucinating. I feel tears making my cheeks wet. After searching for a job for such a long time, I have finally found it.

I want to celebrate. I want to scream at the top of my lungs. I want to share this good news with someone. But who? My mother won't really like to hear from me. I can text one of my friends from the university and they'd probably even pretend to be happy for me but won't really be interested much. They've all moved on with their lives without me and I don't blame them. I guess this is something I should keep to myself.

But I have to do something to celebrate. Perhaps I can go to the city centre tomorrow and go to one of those expensive restaurants.

I also need to buy some nice shirts, some nice trousers and shoes to match. I don't have enough formal clothes. This is my first job and I want to put my best foot forward. I can even buy some groceries near my office because there aren't many grocery stores around me.

I take a deep breath and smile. Before the anxiety sets in again. I've got a job I don't know anything about or I'm interested in. I go back to the website to read more about what I am really supposed to do. I didn't pay much attention to the job description before applying because I was that desperate but now that I will actually have to work, I am nervous.

The project is run by the Scottish History Department and they have hired five research assistants who would research the lives of witches in Scotland and at the end of the year, they would present their findings at a conference held by the university. I only graduated a few months ago, so I don't have enough experience to get this job but if there's one thing I am good at, it's pretending. I can pretend to be good at anything if that's what the situation demands. Right now, I need to pretend that I am good at doing historical research. I guess I can do that. How hard can it be?

That night I sleep peacefully and I don't even have to keep my lights switched on.

***

On September 10th, I reach the History Department and do some remaining paperwork before I can actually start working. Once I am done, I reach the cafeteria fifteen minutes before I am supposed to reach and I am surprised to see Henry already there.

"Oh, good morning." I forgot what Henry looks like but thankfully, he recognises me. When I met Henry for the first time, we were both sitting so I could only see the upper half of his body. But now that I am standing next to him, I can properly observe him. He's only a couple of inches taller than me, which is saying something since I am only 5 feet and 2 inches.

"Good morning, Kali. Nice to see you. Are you excited for your first day?"

"Yes, I am." I pretend I am enthusiastic but I am not. To be honest, I am sleep deprived. Why wouldn't I be? I had to wake at half-past seven this morning just so that I could get dressed and be here on time. My heart breaks a little knowing that I'd have to do this five days a week for the foreseeable future.

I wait with Henry for other research assistants to show up while he offers to buy me a coffee. One by one they appear and hug Henry. It looks to me like they already are close to each other. Employees don't hug their bosses when they meet them.

"Hi." One of the girls waves at me politely. "I am Lisa." She is a short blonde girl talking in a very thick Glaswegian accent. Thankfully, I spent the last week on YouTube learning to understand the Glaswegian accent.

"I am Kali. It looks like all of you know each other already." I chuckle nervously. It feels awkward to be the only new one in the group.

"Oh, yeah. We all worked together on the last project as well. But don't feel left out, okay?"

I nod. Of course, I am feeling left out. I am the only one who is new here.

Henry takes all four of us upstairs and we head to the office where we'll work for the next year. It's more of a study room than an office. There are several computers and desks and there is a vending machine in the corner.

"This used to be a study space for postgraduate students for history doctoral students. In fact, I used to study here," Henry tells us.

I have to admit that I quite like this office. There is an enormous window through which we can see the whole university before us. The chairs look comfortable, there is a machine that dispenses chocolates and the office is warm. I'll be fine here.

Henry asks all of us to introduce ourselves one by one. They all have graduated from the University of Glasgow, which is how they all know each other. I am the only new person in the room. When it is my turn, I introduce myself. "Hi, I am Kali. I just moved from Birmingham to Glasgow and I look forward to working with you all." I give the generic introduction that I prepared before coming here. The four other people who are working with me are Natacha, Esme and Lisa and of course, Henry. Is it a coincidence that all four of us chosen for this job are women? Perhaps. It's a project about witches, after all.

Henry gets up and introduces himself. "Hi, everyone. You all have already met me at the job interview and three of you know me already since we have worked on projects together before, but I am still going to introduce myself." He smiles at me. "I am Henry, the supervisor of the project we are going to work on over the next year. I graduated from this very university about two years ago with a PhD but I didn't feel like leaving so I stayed behind." He turns on the projector and shows all of us a presentation.

"So, this is what we are going to work on. Through this project, we aim to study the lives of women who were called witches in Scotland." He gives all of us a handout and starts to read from the paper out loud.

"The Scottish Parliament criminalised witchcraft in 1563, just before King James's birth. It was a capital offence to be a witch. The first major witchcraft panic arose in 1590 after nearly three decades passed. King James was made to believe that he and his Danish bride, Anne, had been attacked by witches who brought dangerous storms upon them to try to kill the royals during their voyages across the North Sea.

"King James sanctioned witch trials after an alarming confession in 1591 from Agnes Sampson, who was an accused witch. It was revealed that 200 witches—even some from Denmark—had sailed in sieves to the church of the coastal town of North Berwick on Halloween night in 1590. There the devil preached to them and encouraged them to plot the King's destruction. After hearing these confessions, even though they had been extorted by torture, King James and his advisers believed a witchcraft conspiracy threatened his reign.

"It was this incident that led to fear and panic among the common people over the next century. A total number of 3,837 people were accused of witchcraft in Scotland, 85% of them were women. About 67% were executed.

"A common practice to test if a woman was a witch or not was known as witch pricking. The accused was pricked by a sharp needle, if she did not bleed or hurt, it was believed that the accused was marked by the devil and was proclaimed a witch.

"The accused women were brutally tortured and often confessed to their crimes to put an end to their suffering. The women were often burnt at the stake so that their dead bodies couldn't be possessed by the devil."

He looks up from the paper and waits for any of us to respond. When nobody does, I decide to speak. "That's horrible." And it is horrible indeed. I read about all of this just last night so I wouldn't totally be lost at the job. And still hearing this again gives me chills. Imagine burning women just because you don't like them.

Henry nods. "Yes. Through this project, we want to shed some light on the lives of these women and hope we can bring them some sort of justice." He starts the presentation. "So, how we are going to do it is we will focus on the lives of five witches. All five of them are from different periods of time and through them, we are going to highlight how women were treated. Natacha is going to focus on witches in the 16th century." Natacha nods as if she knew this already. "Esme, 17th century." Esme nods too. "Lisa, 18th century." Lisa responds with a yes. "I am going to do the 19th century. And Kali," he turns to me, "you get the last one. 20th century. Is everyone okay with this?"

Everyone says yes, but I don't say anything. I wish I had got one of the earlier centuries, maybe the 17th or 18th. But I don't want to make a fuss on my very first day, so I don't say anything and nod quietly.

"This one whole week our aim is to find the one witch each of us is going to focus on. On Friday at 4 p.m., we are going to have a meeting right here and I want a name. You are free to use whichever resources you want. The university has an extensive library, there are lots of resources in the British Library and the National Library of Scotland too. You can also go to the archives department if you need anything. Just get your permission slips signed by me and you can access everything. Three of you already know how this works, so I hope you'll help Kali get acquainted with the process as soon as possible." Henry pauses and looks at everyone. "Does anyone have any questions?" he asks, but no one says anything. "Awesome then. Let's get to work."

Everyone grabs a computer, and they begin frantically doing their work. I go to the computer kept in the corner and start to work. But I am overwhelmed. Where do I start? What am I even supposed to do? I Google witches in Scotland in the 20th century and I read through a bunch of links but I don't understand anything. The truth is: I don't know anything about witches in Scotland. In the interview, I pretended that I knew at least the basic details about them after reading through a few Wikipedia pages, and that was enough for Henry to think that I am actually interested in the job.

But now that I have actually got the job, I don't know what to do. I must begin from the beginning.

I am reading through a few research papers on JSTOR when Henry taps my shoulder.

"All well?" He tilts his head.

I want to lie, I don't want to admit that I have no idea what I am supposed to do and run away, but the expression on his face tells me he already knows how good I am feeling right now. "Uh, Henry. I am not sure where to start."

He drags a chair and sits next to me. "Don't worry. This is your first time working on something like this, I understand. Don't be worried. I just emailed you a bunch of research papers that I found and I think you should begin reading them. Just learn about what things were like in those times and come to me if you have any questions."

Alright, I can do this. I can read through a few research papers.

"Don't be overwhelmed." He puts his hand on my shoulder again and takes the computer next to mine. I don't like this. If he were away, I could have easily pretended that I am reading something while actually being on Twitter, but since he is sitting next to me, I have to actually do some work. I check the email that he sent me. When he told me he sent me a 'bunch of research papers', I assumed there'd be five or six of them. But there are 109 research papers attached.

"Do I have to read all of these?"

"Um, you can sift through a few of them and find which ones are helpful." He turns his chair around to look at me. It doesn't seem that 109 is a big number for him.

"Alright."

I take a deep breath and begin reading. It will take me one whole year just to finish reading these essays, I don't know when I'll actually do some research.

Sitting next to Henry, I read through these papers page by page and I have to try really hard to stifle my yawns. When it's lunchtime, I am thankful for a break. A few hours of reading and my brain is almost dead. I don't know how I'll survive the rest of the year.

"Kali, all of us are going to the cafeteria to grab lunch. Would you like to join?" Natacha asks. Saying 'no' to them on the first day at work would be rude so I agree. We all head downstairs and grab a table in the busy cafeteria. I packed my own lunch so I eat my cheese and onion sandwich while the others get themselves fancy food.

"Here, this is for you." Henry puts a large cup of hot chocolate in front of me.

"Oh, thank you. How much is it?" I bend down to take my wallet out of my bag but he stops me.

"It's on me, don't worry about it." He takes a chair next to me and eats his lasagna. I notice he hasn't bought hot chocolate for everyone, it's just for me.

"How is it going so far?" he asks everyone.

It's Esme who responds. "There's a lot of stuff to go through. Like, a lot." I am glad Esme feels the same way as I do. Although I am exceptionally bored and I have only been at work for a few hours. Being a research assistant is harder than I thought it'd be.

"Yeah, there is. But we'd be fine. We have a lot of time. I was wondering if we could go to the archives after lunch where we can explore more," Henry suggests and everyone else in the room nods but me. More boring documents?

"Sounds good, Kali?" Henry turns to me specifically. Everyone looks at me.

"Sounds great!" I smile.

How I survive the rest of the day is something I don't even know. I have to drink three cups of coffee just to keep myself from falling asleep. I stop reading the research papers that Henry sent me and head to the archives along with everyone. I am not sure what I am supposed to be looking through. I browse through shelves to read something exciting, I can't bring myself to read historical journals. I even go far from everyone so that they don't see what I am doing.

I go to the last bookshelf and pick the thinnest book. It's called 'How To Be A Witch'. I turn around to see if anyone's looking at me, but they are not. Good. I take the thin book out and read it through. Did someone really write a manual about how to become a witch? And it ended up in a university's archives? This is hilarious. The book has instructions on how to make different potions, how to hex, how to make voodoo dolls, how to call spirits through the ouija board and so much more.

I wonder if I start doing some of these things written here, will I become a witch? I know I said I am a woman of facts and figures but a little curiosity won't kill the cat. Frankly, I'd love to do magic, but I don't want to sell my soul to Satan or anything. I am not sure if I can even do some of the things written in the book, they are too ghastly. A page mentions that I need to bury a jasmine flower dipped in my own blood in my garden to seek revenge upon a known enemy. Yeah, drawing my own blood would be a great way to seek revenge.

I know I shouldn't be reading this book in the first place. It's all garbage, written for entertainment and nothing else. I can't actually use this book for my research. I am supposed to study the history of the times these witches lived in rather than this.

I find a copy of James VI's copy of *Daemonologie* and read through it while sitting along with everyone. I can't pretend to not work for too long. Henry might even ask me what I have found so far at the end of the day, so I must actually work. And honestly, I start to enjoy my work a little too. Just a little.

I am thankful when the clock hits five, and I am finally free to go home. We leave the archives and gather outside for a quick meeting before we leave. Henry asks us to discuss what we've found so far. I was scared the three girls might have worked harder than me, but no, they are all just as clueless as I am. When it's my turn, I say, "I read through James VI's *Daemonologie*."

"Hmm, that does not directly refer to your research, but it might help you understand the basics," Henry says. "This is great, you're working on your basics. That's good."

I smile, knowing that I did something right. "I also came across a book which seems like a manual to becoming a witch."

"Really? That's interesting. You should perhaps focus more on that if it is a twentieth-century publication."

"Oh, alright." Really? I didn't think that manual would be too helpful but if Henry says I should look into it, I will. Even though it was all bollocks, it was still very entertaining to read. Maybe I'll come across a spell to earn more money. I'd happily draw my blood and dip a flower into it if that means I'll have more money.

Henry claps his hand to get everyone's attention. "Anyway, girls. Good job considering this was our very first day. We'll continue working like this through the rest of the week and decide on a figure we want to focus on this Friday. You are free to leave now." We all mutter goodbye to Henry and leave.

The fresh air hits me right in the face when I step out of the building. What an absolutely boring day with a bunch of boring people. The only highlight of my day was reading that witchy manual. Should I quit my job? No. That would be silly. This job pays handsomely, and as the year progresses, I know it will get less boring. Until then, I must find a way to survive.

Now I think that it's better I am focusing on the 20th century rather than older centuries. At least I would get to read some manuals for my source material. The three girls leave me behind and walk somewhere together. I wish they were friendlier to me. They didn't even say goodbye. I was hoping I'd make friends at work, but that doesn't seem to be happening anytime soon.

I want to celebrate my first day of work in some way, but I don't know anyone else in the city. I also am not ready to go back to my flat all alone just now, so I head to a Subway nearby. Subway is hardly fancy, but it's one of the places where I feel comfortable. I order a six-inch sub along with a cold drink and grab a seat.

Moving to a new city is always difficult, I knew that. Sometimes I wonder if I'd made a silly, impulsive decision, but considering how things were back home, I am glad I am away. I used to still live with my mother while I was at university because I wanted to save money. I did end up saving my rent money, but in the three years that I stayed there, I completely lost my mind.

My mother is a narcissist, to put it politely. I can go on and on about how abusive she has been, but I just don't want to think about her anymore now that I am in a new city. All I will say is that I was emotionally abused for most of my life. That's a long time. I have wasted years of my life not being me just because I wasn't fully able to be myself.

Not anymore. Things will be different now. I am making a new start. I have a new job, I am in a new city and I will be happy again.

I finish my sandwich and head back to my flat. I don't want to be out too late, especially considering where I live.

Once I am back home, I lie down on my bed. This whole job thing is hard. I can't believe I have to do it every day for the rest of my life. I change into my pyjamas and I am preparing my meal for tomorrow when I hear a sound in my backyard. I look through the window and see a black cat staring right back at me. Its eyes twinkle like diamonds in the darkness. It is sitting on the garbage bin meowing at me. I open the door and go near it to see if it is okay. It does seem okay. How did it get here? I look around to see if there's anyone around, but nope.

"Are you someone's pet?" I ask the cat and it tilts its head at me. I don't know why I am talking to a cat and expecting it to answer me.

It doesn't have a collar on either. I shut my door and get back inside. I'll let the cat find its own way back home and get back to cooking. But not even a moment passes and I hear scratching against my door. I open the door and the black cat purrs.

"Shoo," I say but it has no effect on the cat. The girl who sublet me the flat told me that there is a no-pet-policy in the flat.

"I can't take you in," I tell the cat apologetically. It ignores me and gets inside. I look around, I see no humans around me. I shut the door and think to myself. The girl is in Berlin, how would she know I let a cat inside? Unless a neighbour saw me, there's no way she'd find out that there is a cat inside.

Besides, it's too dark and cold for it to spend the night outside alone. I'll find its owner tomorrow. Is it a girl cat, though? I lift its legs up to check but I have no idea how cat anatomy works. I have never had a cat, but from what I have seen so far, cats aren't as friendly as dogs. Holding this cat in my arms makes me miss my Ruby. Whatever its gender, it won't stay with me for long so I don't need to know.

I have never owned a cat before, so I have no idea what I am supposed to do and how to take care of cats. I bring a pillow from my bedroom and put it on the sofa. The cat sniffs at the pillow and then sits on top of it. Okay, good. Now I must find it something to eat. I leave the cat on the sofa and go to the kitchen. A quick Google research tells me I should give it some water, tuna and a warm blanket. I check if I have any tuna in my fridge and thankfully I do. The cat follows me along in the kitchen and meows again. Perhaps it is hungry.

I don't have any bowls specifically for cats, so it's my own breakfast bowl that I put some tuna in. While it eats, I put another bowl of water next to it.

The cat eats the tuna and drinks the water hurriedly. So it indeed was hungry. After eating, it seems much calmer and lies down on the sofa with its eyes closed. It must be tired. I make myself a cup of tea and sit next to it as I watch some TV. It's very calming being in the same room with another living thing, but I also don't want to get used to this feeling. The cat's owner must be looking for it right now.

I take my laptop and go to the missing cats Facebook group to see if someone's lost a black cat. I see no such posts. Although I'd love to keep it with me, it wouldn't be right for me to keep it away from its real home. The cat is quite comfortable sleeping on the sofa and isn't scared or quiet. It has taken very well to its surroundings, I did not know cats were so comfortable in new places. Ruby always wreaked havoc whenever we took her to a new place. Perhaps cats are different.

I wake up in the middle of the night on the sofa and realise I must have fallen asleep. The cat is asleep next to me too. I leave it on the sofa and head to my bed. I have to wake up early tomorrow again for work.

In the morning, the cat wakes me up before my alarm does. It is sitting on my stomach and meowing. I check the time, it's only five minutes before my alarm is about to go off so I am not too mad at this black void. What am I going to do with it? Should I just leave it alone in my flat? That doesn't seem right. I'll leave it outside for it to find its way back home.

I get dressed and put some tuna and water in bowls again. When the cat has done eating, I put it outside my flat at the same place I found it last night. It might be able to find its way back home, or maybe its owner would find it today. It's not cold during the day, and it is likely the cat's owner must be looking for it. It should be fine. I rush to the subway to catch my train.

My second day at work is marginally better than it was yesterday. While yesterday I spent the whole day understanding what I am even supposed to do, today I have a better idea of how things work. I go to the library and find a book on modern witches and leaf through it.

"Found anything interesting?" Henry asks as he puts his hand on my shoulder. Is it necessary for him to touch me whenever he wants my attention?

I turn around. "I have just started reading this book I got from the library and I hope I'll find something."

"Let me know if you have any trouble, okay?"

"Sure."

Henry leaves me alone in peace as he moves on to talk to Natacha. I have to admit that the book I am currently reading is both interesting and horrifying at the same time. I am just glad I was not born at a time when they were killing women for no reason at all. I read through the book and read through the documents online. Henry mentioned that each of us has to choose one woman to focus on. When he said that, I thought I would struggle to choose, but I am not confused at all.

I come across a woman called Isabella Gowdie who was called a witch by her neighbours. According to several sources, she was one of the most dangerous witches in history, although she wasn't burnt at the stake because it was illegal at the time. Nonetheless, she remained a mysterious figure. I look at her photo in the book and see nothing scary about her. She looks like a nice woman with a smile on her face. She is wearing a pretty red dress with flowers on it. This is not how I imagined witches look like. I read about her for the rest of the day, and each and every source is even more interesting than the last one.

I find a blog that discusses these witches and some people have pointed out that she was suffering from 'hysteria' and according to some people, she was a sexually promiscuous woman and of course, that would get you labelled as a witch. From what I've read so far, I find her an interesting woman, a woman I'd like to know more about for the rest of the year. It'd be interesting to find out if she was hysterical or horny or just a woman with desires.

I hope Henry approves of her. I spend the next few hours preparing a list of resources I am going to use while doing my research. I pick up a few research papers that Henry emailed me, a few books from the library, and I even put the name of the blog I was just reading. Official resources are one thing, but actually seeing what people are talking about can be important too.

In the evening, when I am about to leave, Henry comes to me, "Some of us are going to the pub to get some drinks this Friday, would you like to join us?"

"Sure." I haven't gone out for drinks with people in ages and besides, this can be a good opportunity for me to get to know my colleagues more.

Once I have left the office, I don't waste my time loitering around the city because I want to get to my flat as soon as possible. If that cat is still there, I would have to feed it. Although I hope its owner was able to find the cat.

When I get back to my flat, it isn't there in my backyard. I'd like to think that its owner indeed found it. I sigh and go back inside. Deep down, I wished the cat was still here outside. It was good company for me since I live alone.

When I was looking for flats in Glasgow, I was struggling since I went to so many viewings and yet I couldn't find anything suitable and affordable. However, the girl who owns this flat was subletting it for six months and she let me keep it without much hassle. She was desperately looking for a tenant and I was desperately looking for a flat, so this situation worked for both of us. I didn't need to buy anything when I came here, just my two suitcases that fit all my twenty-two years of existence. But I feel terribly lonely here. I would have adopted a cat of my own, but I don't want to leave her alone while I am away.

I go to my kitchen to eat my staple dinner of cup noodles when I see the cat right outside my flat. I leave everything and rush out to get it inside.

"So, you didn't find your owner?" I ask the cat, but it ignores me. I have decided that I am going to call the cat 'her' because calling the cat 'it' doesn't sound very nice if she's going to stay with me for at least one more day. I hold her in my arms and she lays her head against my breast. She looks hungry and cold. Now I feel bad for leaving her alone. I bring her inside and she goes to my sofa and lies down on a pillow. I am glad she is making herself at home. I check my Facebook group one more time to see if there are any posts about looking for her. I don't find anything and so I decide to mail my local cat shelter home instead. I get a response within twenty minutes. "We are sorry, but we haven't received any complaints about a lost black cat. We'd let you know if we do get one. Meanwhile, I have put the cat's photo on our website and Facebook page. Maybe someone will come forward."

"No one's looking for you?" I ask the cat, but she looks at me in confusion. I need to feed her. I don't have any tuna fish in my fridge anymore. I give her a bowl of water, but obviously, that isn't enough for her. She must be famished. I take her in my arms and give her a kiss on her forehead. "Let's get you some food." I wear my jacket, take her in my arms and head out.

There's not much near me where I live. No Tesco or Sainsbury's or even Lidl. Although there's an Iceland store where I might find something for her. It's a cloudy day outside and it was even sprinkling a few hours ago. Leaving this cat out alone was a mistake, a big mistake.

"You can't take your cat inside," the guard outside Iceland stops me.

"But where else would I leave her?" He only shrugs. "If I leave her here, would you take care of her for a while? I'll be back soon."

"Taking care of cats is not my job, lady." The man is rude. Now, I am confused. I would like to buy a carrier for the cat, but even for that, I need to go inside the store. As I am mulling over, the cat jumps from my arms and deposits herself in one of the trolleys. The guard looks displeased but doesn't say anything.

I go inside the store leaving her outside in the trolley and quickly buy a litter box, some cat food, a little toy and a carrier for her. I don't know how long I'd be able to keep her, but no matter how long she is with me, I'd like to make her feel comfortable. Maybe when I find her owner, I can give them this stuff.

When I come outside, the cat is no longer there.

"Where's my c—" I ask the guard, but I stop midway when I find her sitting in the middle of a road outside the store. What the hell is she doing there? There are no cars, so she's safe for now. I rush to get her, but with so much stuff in my hands, I struggle to hold her in my arms. I drop her bag of cat food and when I bend down to pick it up, I feel something coming towards me. I look up and see a car only a few metres away. I know I should take the cat, leave all the stuff that I have, and run. But I am frozen in shock. A scream comes out of me and the car stops only a few inches away from me.

"Are you alright, hen?" a middle-aged woman steps out of the car and runs towards me. I am too shocked to respond, so I simply nod. She helps me get my stuff and takes me to the side of the road. I sit on the sidewalk and breathe. The cat jumps into my lap and rubs her head against my stomach. I can see she is trying to calm me down. The woman gets back in her car, parks it on the side and then comes to me.

"Are you sure you're alright?" she asks again. I look up to see her and she is genuinely worried about me.

"I am fine, really." My answer doesn't satisfy her.

"Where do you live? Can I drop you somewhere?"

"No, I only live a ten-minute walk away. I will be fine on my own." She doesn't respond and continues looking at me in pity. I look around, I have too much stuff to carry and actually, a lift to my house would be welcome. "Actually, it would be great if you can help me carry my stuff to my flat."

She nods, and a smile appears on her face. She takes all the stuff from me and carries it to her car. I only have the cat in my arms. We reach my flat in about five minutes.

"Would you like to come inside and have a cup of tea?" I ask her. She has helped me and I must find a way to thank her.

"Sure." I am surprised she isn't worried about having a cup of tea with a stranger.

As I am making some tea in the kitchen, she sits with the cat in the living room.

"I hope you won't mind me asking, but what were you doing in the middle of the road? God forbid if I hadn't stopped in time..." She doesn't finish her sentence and only shakes her head with her eyes closed.

"It's my fault, you shouldn't blame yourself. My cat ran and sat in the middle of the street and I ran after her. I asked the guard to take care of her and he just didn't listen to me."

"You should not take your cat to grocery stores, didn't you know this?"

"This is only my second day with this cat, she is not even my cat. I just found her in the backyard and I have to go find her owner now. Maybe I should try putting posters in the neighbourhood."

The lady sips her tea. "Have you considered the possibility that the cat might have been abandoned?"

She is right. I never thought of it this way. "You might be right. I don't know why I didn't think of it." I take the poor cat in my arms. "Who would abandon their pet just like that?"

"Tons of people do that. I used to run a shelter for animals, actually. You can't imagine the things people have done to their pets."

"Oh." Should I put this cat in a shelter? No, I don't want to do that. Maybe I'll just adopt her.

"By the way, I am Betty."

"Hello, I am sorry I didn't even introduce myself. I am Kali."

"What a beautiful name. Have you lived here long, Kali? My son just lives a few doors down and I was coming to meet him."

"I just moved to Glasgow last month." There's no point in lying to her like I usually lie in my interviews.

"Oh, so you are new to the city. Do you have a lot of friends here?" she asks as she takes a sip of the tea.

"None, actually." I don't like the way Betty is looking at me right now, so I swiftly say, "Although I started a new job this week, so hopefully, I'll make friends soon." I force a smile.

"I know this might sound strange to you, but I'd love to stay in touch with you. I live alone too, just like you. My son does visit me every weekend, but I am alone most of the week. I'd love to be of help to you. Maybe I can help you with taking care of your cat."

"Oh, that sounds lovely." I had heard of Glaswegian hospitality before, but I wasn't expecting people to be this nice to me already.

Betty and I spend the next hour chatting about cats. She tells me little anecdotes about cats in her shelter, and I don't even realise when the hour passes by. She gives me her phone number and takes mine too before leaving.

"Call me whenever you need to ask anything about cats or are just feeling lonely."

"I will, thank you," I feel warm inside when I say this.

I look at my cat, and she blinks back at me. I don't know how long I'd be able to keep her with me, but as long as I have her, I need to give her a name. "What should I call you?" She ignores me and perches on my bed with her eyes closed. I go into the kitchen to make some dinner for myself when I see a jar of olives. Olive sounds like a good name. She even looks like a pitted black olive.

I go back to my bedroom. "From today, I'll call you Olive." She gives me no sign of approval and I go back to the kitchen.

I won't lie, I have never been fond of cats. I was always a dog person, they are friendly. But there's just something about Olive that makes me feel protective of her. Even if she ignores me all the time, I am glad I am not alone in my flat right now.

***

On the first day of work, I was completely bored but as Friday comes around, I actually started enjoying myself. I realise that this job is better than many jobs. During university, I worked as a waitress and was paid a quarter of what I am earning right now. This is exactly why I don't want to take this job for granted. Sure, I have to read a lot but that's much better than cleaning up after dirty people in restaurants.

Henry seems to be really proud of what I have done so far. "You are really fast. You've already narrowed down your research and you know who you want to focus on. Great job." He pats me on the back. These words of encouragement mean a lot to me.

Henry calls for a meeting at 4 p.m. where we all gather around the table to discuss what we have found so far. Natacha, Esme and Lisa talk about what they have found and then it's my turn. I clear my throat and start to speak. "I am going to focus on Isabella Gowdie who is arguably the last witch of Scotland." They all nod at me as if they approve of the witch I have chosen to focus on. I continue, "She was born in 1921 and there are several sources that claim that she was a witch. She was famous for doing magic with voodoo dolls and she died under mysterious circumstances after a priest locked her down in her hut." I stop talking and look at Henry.

"She seems interesting. I look forward to reading more about what you find." I smile at him. I like that Henry is impressed with my work.

"Alright, then. We have worked hard this week and we need to celebrate our work. Does anyone have any suggestions for where we should go?"

Esme speaks, "How about the Haunted House since we are studying witches?" The others cheer at Esme's suggestion. Since I am new to the city, I have nothing to add to the discussion.

The Haunted House doesn't look haunted to me at all when we grab a table. Sure, it's dark and there are skulls on the walls but they need to do better with their decorations. Henry buys our first round and gets me a glass of cider I haven't tasted before.

"What is it?" I ask as I take a sip. While I do not enjoy drinking ciders a lot, this is actually good.

"A good old Scottish cider. Do you like it?" he asks.

"I love it."

While I have known my colleagues for a week now, I haven't actually spoken at length with any of them and I'd love to know them more. But the problem is all four of them already know each other and I feel a little left out.

"Where are you from, Natacha?" I ask when Esme and Lisa go to the toilet and I finally get a chance to speak.

"I am from Uddingston, but I live right here in the West End."

"Is Uddingston far from here?"

"Oh, no. Less than an hour by train but I wanted to move out so I am here. Where do you live?"

"I live in Govan."

"Govan?" Henry jumps in.

"Yeah, why? Is there something wrong with it?"

Natacha and Henry both look at each other. "There's nothing really wrong with Govan, it's just not the best place to live in

Glasgow. You're new to the city, right? What made you find a flat there?"

"I was just desperate to find a flat, and that's all I could find."

Esme and Lisa return now and Natacha tells them I live in Govan as if it is the latest hot piece of gossip. "Why do you live in Govan?" There's disgust on Esme's face.

"Come on, Esme. She is new to Glasgow, she doesn't know anything."

I know Govan is not the best place to live but I still don't like the way they are talking right now. "What's wrong with Govan?"

Henry answers my question. "Lots of criminals live there, people who are addicted to stuff and some religious fanatics. Also, there's a football stadium. I suggest you don't take the subway when there's a football match between Celtics and Rangers. The sports fans can get violent."

I nod slowly, taking in whatever Henry is saying. "I am only subletting so I won't be there for a long time. I'll get a flat somewhere else, somewhere nicer."

"Oh, that's cool. You can just move to the city centre or West End." I nod.

Esme gets a phone call, and she leaves us taking Lisa along with her. Natacha finishes her drink and says, "I should head out too. I'll see you guys on Monday."

I still have half of my drink left so I have to wait for a while. Thankfully, Henry stays on to give me some company. "Do you have any plans for the weekend?" he asks.

"Not really. I was thinking of maybe exploring the city. Or maybe I'll just sleep for the next two days."

Henry laughs. "Would you like to have another drink? I am not ready to go home just yet."

I look at my now-empty glass of cider. "Sure, let's drink."

Henry returns this time with two glasses of Vodka lime soda. "Thought we need something stronger now."

"You should have let me get this round, you bought the last round too."

"Oh, don't worry. You can get the next two rounds." Next two rounds? I don't think I'd like to stay here for that long but I quietly sip my drink.

Now that all the girls are gone and I have some alcohol within me, I am feeling more comfortable. "So, you're from Birmingham?" Henry asks.

"Yeah, lived there all my life."

"I am from Blackpool but I moved here after school. Don't think I'd ever go back."

"You like Glasgow so much?"

"It's a pretty cool city. What about you? Would you like to go back?"

I don't even have to think for a second to respond. "Not at all, Henry. I might move somewhere else but I am not ready to go back to Birmingham just yet."

Even though Henry is my supervisor, it's awfully easy to talk to him. I am pretty sure he is only a few years older than me. He has a PhD though which is why he has landed the job he currently has. While I had initially told myself I wouldn't have two more rounds of drinks with him, I end up staying.

"I think we should call it a night," I tell Henry after I finish my fourth drink. My words are starting to slur and I have reached the point where I can't drink anymore without puking my guts out.

"Sure, let's go. I think I should escort you back home. It's a Friday night, there'd be lots of drunk guys in Govan."

"Don't worry about me, Henry. I don't live that far from the subway station."

"You sure?"

"Yes, I am sure."

I get up and take a second to steady myself. Henry seems to be in a much better condition than me. He helps me wear my jacket and we both walk outside.

"At least let me walk you to the subway?" he asks and I can't deny his offer.

"Sure." I smile at him. I like him so far. I have had a history of having awful bosses but Henry just might be different.

"Do you really like this job?" Henry's question takes me aback.

I stutter before responding. "Of course I do. I know I am still getting the hang of things but I've enjoyed working here so far."

Henry smiles at me as if he knows something I don't know. I don't think he actually believes me. I was right, Henry is really good at reading people.

"What about you? Do you like this job?" I ask.

"I do. I am very passionate about everything history. This is important stuff, you know?"

I nod. We finally reach the subway station. "Thanks for walking me here, will you be okay going home yourself?"

"Yeah, don't worry about me. I'll see you soon." He turns around and waves a goodbye at me.

When I come outside the train station, it's pretty dark outside. I look for the paper cutter in my bag that I usually keep but it's not there anymore. I must have taken it out sometime during the week. My flat is exactly a ten-minute walk away, eight if I speed walk. I say a little prayer and go outside the station.

As I am walking, I feel somebody behind me but when I turn around, there's no one. I don't have time to think if there was actually somebody behind me. I just put one leg in front of the other. It's pretty windy outside and now I regret staying out for drinks this late. I suddenly feel something on my back, as if someone's put their hand on my shoulder to stop me. I turn around but once again there's no one behind me. I turn around and this time I don't walk, I run to my flat.

My heart is hammering against my chest once I am finally inside my building. I look outside through the glass door to see if anyone has followed me behind. I see no one. I head up to my flat and breathe a sigh of relief. I am still scared but once I am in my bed, Olive comes and sits next to me and I feel okay again.

Chapter 2

I wake up the next day at 12 p.m. because I ended up bingeing a show on Netflix last night after I got home. I was still shaken by my eight-minute walk last night and I was completely smashed. I didn't want to go to bed because over the years I have noticed that I get sleep paralysis whenever I am completely smashed and it felt like I was going to get one of those episodes last night. After drinking three cups of coffee back to back, I fell asleep after 5 a.m. this morning.

But I don't want to waste the rest of my day. I Google 'things to do in Glasgow' but I can't figure out what to do. I look at Olive, but she is softly snoring in her sleep. I wish I could be a cat sometimes.

Half the day passes once I have showered and eaten something and then it's too late to go out anywhere. Maybe I'll do something fun tomorrow. I can even go outside Glasgow, maybe I can make a quick day trip to the Scottish Highlands. Today I continue to stay in my flat and binge-watch another TV show. I am comfortable in my bed when I hear someone knocking on my door.

At first, I think it's my annoying neighbour who keeps asking me for an iPhone charger even though I have told her multiple times that I don't have an iPhone but I am surprised to see Betty standing before me.

"I am sorry I dropped by without letting you know I was coming. I was just passing by," she says apologetically.

"Oh, don't worry, Betty. Come in." There is a man with her who I am assuming is her son. They look nothing alike though. While Betty is a tiny woman who can't be taller than five feet, the man next to her is towering over me.

I let both of them in. Olive comes out to see who has come to visit and when she sees it's Betty, she comes to greet her. I am surprised to see Olive being so friendly with strangers. Maybe she's a friendly cat and it's just me who she doesn't like.

"She seems to like you more than me," I comment as I take both of their jackets and hang them behind the door.

Betty laughs. "All animals love me. Anyway, this is my son Hans. We were both passing by and then I was reminded that you don't have this."

She hands me a bag. I take a peek inside and see a few bottles inside. "What are these, Betty?"

"It is a special oil for cats to keep their fur healthy."

"Oh, thank you for bringing it. I bought Olive a litter tray but there are still so many things I need to learn to take care of her properly."

"Don't worry, Kali. You'll learn quickly. Taking care of a cat is not that difficult."

"Would you like something to drink? Tea or coffee?" I offer while thinking that I have neither in my flat. I drank all my coffee last night and I don't think I've ever even bought tea.

Betty looks at her son and then at me. "Oh, no. We shouldn't ruin your Saturday."

"You're not ruining my Saturday. I wasn't doing anything, anyway."

"You should be going out and having fun, Kali," she says to me while rubbing her hand on my shoulders. For some reason, her touch feels exactly like the touch I felt last night while walking home from the station. But then I was so drunk last night, I am not even sure if someone actually touched me yesterday or if I imagined all of that.

I shrug. Betty turns to Hans, "Kali is new in the city so she doesn't know many people."

"I'll be fine, Betty. Don't worry about me."

"I don't live too far from you, if you ever want to hang out with me and my friends," Hans speaks to me for the first time. I observe him. Hans is undeniably cute. He's tall and quite well-built. He is very attractive, I have to admit. Being in his presence makes me nervous. He looks like the kind of lad who bullied other kids in their teenage years. A good-looking, bad boy. But it's his eyes that draw me towards him. There's something special about them.

Betty and Hans agree to stay for a few more minutes. I offer them some coke and biscuits because that's all I had with me. Thankfully, they don't seem to mind. At least the biscuits that I offer them are quite fancy. I bought them the day I found out I had finally got the job.

Hans is observing my living room while Betty is playing with Olive.

"Is Hans a German name?" I ask when he is observing the bookcase of the girl whose flat I am subletting.

Hans smiles and turns to his mother, "You should tell her why you named me Hans."

Betty puts her tea and saucer down. "Hans's father is Irish and I am Scottish. We named him Hans because we were on our honeymoon in Hamburg. We love Germany and we were even hoping to move there when..." She pauses.

"When?" I ask.

Hans continues his mother's story, "When my father died."

"Oh, I am so sorry." There is an awkwardness around the room as there usually is when such matters are talked about.

"Don't be." Betty waves her hand as if she doesn't mind. It seems her husband must've passed recently the way she looks at me. There is a sadness in her eyes that I see reflected in Hans's eyes too.

"Tell us about your name. I haven't met many Kalis in my life," Betty says. I am glad she's changed the topic and we don't have to talk about deaths anymore.

"Well, my parents are Indians and they moved to London and then Birmingham for their jobs. I am named after a Hindu goddess."

"Interesting. I have always wanted to visit India, I just finished reading a book set in India," Betty says.

"Mom is part of a book club she is obsessed with. She never misses a meeting," Hans says.

"After Hans's father passed away, my book club friends make me feel less lonely. Hans doesn't live with me either. He moved away because he wanted to live with his fiancée."

Hans is engaged? Of course, he is. Any man that I am attracted to is either taken or gay. Of course, Hans wouldn't be single either. I politely smile not knowing what to say. I want to know more about his fiancée, but I also don't want to be intrusive.

"Maybe I should join one of those book clubs too, it would give me something to look forward to," I say with a chuckle.

I am only joking about my loneliness but both of them take me seriously and look at me in pity.

"You can always go for a coffee with me," Hans says and I feel my cheeks warming up.

"That'd be nice as long as your fiancée doesn't mind."

"I am single now, my fiancée broke up with me."

"Oh, I am sorry." Now I feel stupid.

"Don't be, she was a dreadful girl," Betty says while scratching Olive's head.

"Dreadful?" I can't help but ask. I am intrigued; very, very intrigued.

Hans sighs. "She just knew how I felt about her and she used it to her advantage. Anyway, I have moved on now."

"Have you?" Betty asks.

"Yes, Mom. I have. Anyway, Kali. You must come with me for a coffee some time. As a friend. I'll show you around Glasgow, it's a beautiful city. We can even go to some cat-friendly restaurants and take Olive with us."

"That would be lovely, Hans."

"Alright, we must leave now. I have to finish reading my book for the book club meeting. Goodbye, Kali. Take care of yourself and take care of Olive."

"I will."

Hans turns around and winks at me as he leaves. What was that for?

***

On Sunday, I decide to head out and explore a little bit of the city by myself. I put Olive in her carrier and since I have a cat with me, I don't take the subway. Walking it is, then.

I walk for a while exploring Govan. Is Govan as bad as people make it seem to be or is there anything worth seeing here? I check Google and first head to Elder Park. It's an ordinary, small green park but there's a small pond with ducks swimming inside. I sit on a bench admiring the view when I hear some lads running and shouting around. They are far from me but when they see me looking at them, they start howling like dogs. I have no idea what they are doing but I leave the park then. I don't want to be around rowdy boys.

The next thing Google suggests I should do is visit the church behind my flat. I am not Catholic but I guess it's something I can do. I don't know if they let cats inside or not though. It's the house of god, every living being should be welcome inside.

The Govan Old Parish Church has an official website, and it says, "Discover the unique collection of early medieval stones carved in the 9th–11th centuries to commemorate the power of those who ruled the Kingdom of Strathclyde."

There are stones outside the church and a closer look at them tells me they are marking some graves. Who was buried here? Just being around these stones is making me feel horrible so I turn around. I don't want to be surrounded by dead people even if they are buried underground.

There's nothing else to do in Govan. It really is a boring area and I must move away from here as soon as possible. While Govan is boring, the rest of the city of Glasgow is quite pretty. I take an Uber and find myself in the West End. I haven't explored this area much. I work inside the office and leave but the area surrounding the university is beautiful.

I find myself a bench in Kelvingrove Park and let Olive out of her carrier for a while. She sniffs the air and claws at my leg, making me put her back again in my lap. What a dumb cat. I am letting her out and instead of enjoying the freedom, she wants to sit like a baby in my arms. It is a cold day outside and perhaps she just wants warmth.

I notice there is a big bouquet of flowers kept on the bench. Why? Did someone leave their flowers after a date? I look around and see there are flowers on almost every bench in the park. There is a couple next to my bench who is softly crying on each other's shoulders. And then it hits me. These flowers are left by someone who was mourning someone's death. I turn around and see a small rectangle on the bench with the words "In memory of our beloved mother, Isabella…"

I hold the flowers in my hands and Olive sniffs at them. "Don't try to eat them, Olive. They are kept here by someone mourning the loss of their mother." Why is death following me around everywhere? First those gravestone markers around the church and now these flowers. I stay in the park for a while and click some pictures of Olive along with the flowers. She is a very photogenic cat and would definitely help me earn a few more followers on Instagram. I am taking her photo when she stands up on the bench and stares at a distance. I follow her gaze and find a woman standing far away. With so much distance between us, it's hard to really see her but I can tell she's looking back at us.

"Olive, do you know her? Is that your owner?"

Olive looks at me and purrs. I have no idea what she means. When I look up again at the woman, she has disappeared. Strange.

I leave the park and take Olive to the vet. I know I might not be able to keep her with me for long but I still want to make sure she has everything that she needs. I also need to check if she's been chipped.

The vet assures me she is fine but he doesn't find a chip. Even he agrees that it's likely that Olive has been abandoned. I take her back home in an Uber. I think my finding Olive is destiny. She was alone, and I was alone and now we have each other. I am also glad that I found her after I got a job because now I can actually take care of her.

Being abandoned and not having a family that can fulfil your emotional needs is the worst. I can understand what Olive is going through. It's something I have gone through myself. Once I am inside, I give Olive her food and a special treat that I bought only for special occasions. It may not be a special occasion today but I just want to love Olive. I want her to know that even if no one comes for her, she'd be safe and loved here under my roof as long as I can take care of her.

On Monday, I leave her alone in the flat with enough food, water and a clean litter tray. The vet assured me that cats, unlike dogs, can be left alone in the house for a while. I am glad I found an abandoned cat, not a dog.

Henry is in a chirpier mood than usual when I reach the office. Before all of us head to our computers, he calls a meeting. "Let's discuss our goals for this week," he says.

"I need to go to the National Library to get some resources," Natacha says.

"Yeah, me too," Esme says. Oh god, I do not want to go to a library at all. They are boring and I'd much rather read on my computer rather than read old, dusty books in the library.

"I think all of us should head there. They have some amazing resources in the archives section. I am sure we'd find something helpful," Henry says.

I sigh and get ready to take my bag with me when Henry comes to me. "Kali, I have something I want to show you."

"What is it, Henry?"

"I looked up Isabella Gowdie and came across a website that mentions where she lived. I think it'd be great if you visit it." I know what Henry is talking about, I came across that website too but I am not too keen to visit the place. I thought this job involved only reading some documents and writing, I don't want to do field research but I don't know what to tell Henry.

"You want me to visit this place this week?"

"Yes. In fact, why not visit it today? You're studying 20th-century witches and I think you'd find more information at this place than in the library." Henry does have a point, and I don't have a valid reason to say no to him.

"Alright, I'll visit it today."

"Cool. Keep a record of all the expenses and you can claim them at the end of the month."

I see all four of them leave, leaving me behind all alone in the office. Sigh. I am not sure if I like working alone.

I go back to the computer to revisit the website that Henry mentioned. Honestly, it's not even a reliable website. It's just a blog managed by a girl who believes witches are real and she even claims to be one. She has a whole section on Isabella Gowdie and the coven she belonged to. Their coven used to gather in a secluded area right outside the city where it is rumoured Isabella Gowdie used to live.

A few other websites mention the hut is haunted, but I quickly shut them. Henry will make me visit the hut no matter what happens, so it's better if I don't read such silly rumours about it. I note down the address and head there.

I have to take a train to reach there and then walk for another thirty minutes to find the hut. I realise that since I am not going to stay in the office all day, I can take Olive with me. At least, that's the positive side of this field research. I rush to my flat, put Olive in her pet carrier and take the train again to Luss where Isabella lived.

Surprisingly, Isabella's hut is mentioned on Google maps. I expected better from a haunted hut. At least witches should have hidden it on maps with their magic. I laugh, thinking I almost believed that the hut is haunted.

From the outside, it just looks dirty and broken down. There's nothing special about it, nothing that would tell me that a witch used to live here. It's covered all around by trees and if it wasn't for Google maps, I would have missed it.

I go inside and find it is even smaller than it looks from the outside. There's nothing inside the hut except a dirty bed, an even dirtier bathroom and a large mirror, almost the size of a tall human. Isabella must have been vain to want such a big mirror for herself. I have no idea what Henry expected me to find here except dirt. I bend down to look under the bed and only see some insects crawling. Disgusting. I take Olive outside her carrier and she looks around inspecting the new location she is in.

I look around the mirror to see if there's anything worth inspecting. I see a large box kept behind it, I open it to see what's inside. I find a diary, a few vials of liquid that looks like water and some dried flowers. I take out the vials to inspect what the liquid is for when Olive jumps at me and I accidentally break the vial in my hand. Oh, no. "Olive, look what you did." I put the box down and smack my hand to get rid of all the glass pieces. I don't even know what kind of liquid it is but whatever it is, I don't want it on me. There is no source of water in the hut so I put the box down and come outside with Olive. I saw a small loch on my way and I go back there to wash my hands.

By the time I reach the loch, my hand starts to burn as if it is on fire. I put my hand in the water, hoping it would soothe the burn but nothing happens. I need to rush to the doctor. I don't think I'll find a doctor here in the wilderness, I have to go back to the city. I wrap my scarf around my hand and hop back on the train.

By the time I am back in the city, the burning sensation is gone. But I still visit a doctor just in case I dropped something poisonous on myself.

"It's nothing to worry about, old dirty water can do that sometimes," the doctor assures me.

"Thank you, I was starting to get worried."

I come back to the office with Olive to write about what I have learnt so far today when I realise that I left the diary and the box behind. Now I have to go back to that dirty hut to get it. It's already 4 p.m. so there's no way I am going there right now since I only work till 5. I wonder if I'd be able to claim my expenses if I go there twice. I hope so.

I spend the next hour lazily describing the hut in my report and staring at the clock waiting for it to hit 5. I know there's no one here but me and Olive, and I can leave early but I don't want to do that. I am glad I don't leave early because Henry comes back around 4:30 p.m.

"Oh, you're back. How was it? Did you find anything?" Henry asks.

"Yeah, I did," I tell him about the secluded hut but I don't tell him that I accidentally left the box in the hut. I don't want him to think I was silly enough to leave such an important artefact behind.

"That's great. I think your research would be much more interesting than any of ours."

I chuckle but I don't reply. "Oh, is that a cat?" He points to my pet carrier.

"Um, yeah. I hope you don't mind I brought her to the office."

"No, problem. Although if any of the senior professors see her, they'd be mad. Keep her hidden and you'll be fine." He bends down on the floor to take a closer look at Olive.

"Do you want me to take her out?" I say when I see that he is curious about Olive.

"Sure."

I take Olive out but she refuses to come outside of the carrier. I don't think she likes Henry very much.

"I'll let you get back to work. Perhaps Olive is just being shy right now," he says.

I thought she'd be friendly with strangers, considering how friendly she was with Betty and Hans, almost as if she has known them all along. I know for sure that she isn't being shy right now, she is just being moody. But I don't say anything. I get back to my computer to finish my report. When it's almost time for me to leave, I mail it to Henry. When the clock hits 5 p.m., I leave.

Back in my flat, Olive swiftly jumps out of her carrier and lies sprawled on the carpet playing with my pillow. Her sharp nails tear apart the fabric and some cotton peaks out of it.

"Olive, no. That's my favourite pillow." Olive leaves my pillow alone and goes back to my bed.

I look into my fridge to see what I can cook for dinner when I see I don't have a lot of groceries left. Unlike last time, I leave Olive alone in my flat and head to Iceland. The guard outside the grocery store is not the same as last time. I wish he was, I would have liked to scold him for not taking care of my cat.

Inside the store, I grab some spaghetti when someone taps on my shoulder and I turn around.

"Hans?" I am shocked to see him here.

"Hey." I almost forgot how cute Hans is. It's been a while since I have been on a date, I haven't even spoken to a man ever since I moved to Glasgow. It'd be nice to have someone in my life.

"What are you doing here?"

"Getting some milk." He lifts the milk jug and shows it to me. How silly I am. Of course, he is in a grocery store to buy his groceries.

"Do you live somewhere near?" His mother did say that she was visiting her son in the neighbourhood but I am not sure if Hans lives close enough to me.

"Yeah, I live on Mckechnie Street, just two doors down from you."

"Really? Why didn't you tell me this the last time?"

"I did tell you. Remember?"

"No, I don't. Well, I am glad to know that you are my neighbour."

"Yeah, see you around." I see him paying for his groceries at the self-checkout and then leaving. I have to admit that Hans looks very cute and his Scottish brawl is adorable. It would be nice to know him more.

The next day I buy another train ticket to Luss where the witch's hut is. I inform Henry that I have to go back to the hut as I want to write something about it and he happily agrees. My train leaves at 9 a.m. so I don't go to the office and head to Luss straight away leaving Olive behind. She is too naughty and can't be trusted. It's better to leave her behind.

I pass by the same loch to reach the hut but this time there are people around me.

"Where are you going?" a woman asks. I find it weird that a stranger is asking me about my whereabouts but I respond anyway.

"I am a researcher from the University of Glasgow, I am writing a research report on the woman who used to live here." I point to the hut.

"You mean the witch who lives here?" The woman's eyebrows pull down together.

"Uh, yeah."

"You can't go inside, it's prohibited." She points to a sign outside the hut which I somehow didn't see yesterday. It clearly says 'entry prohibited'.

"But why?" I don't tell the woman I have already been inside. It seems she wouldn't be too pleased if she finds that out.

"Because the priest trapped the witch inside, if you open the door, you'll set her free." I blink at the woman wondering if she's joking or not.

"Surely you don't believe in such superstitions."

"Aye, I do. So does everyone in this town. It'd be better you stay away too, lass. The witch that lives here preys on young women like you. She'd try to force you to join her coven." The woman looks scared. She has grey hair and pale skin. Being in fear all the time would make anyone look like that.

I struggle to not laugh. "Would you be willing to have a chat with me? About the witch who used to live here?" I am not sure what I am going to find while talking to her but now that I am here, I may as well talk to her. Henry did suggest that I should observe the surroundings around the hut.

"The witch who lives here," the woman interrupts me.

Present tense. She is using the present tense. Either she is completely bonkers or... Or what? What else could be the possibility? Perhaps I am starting to get mad too.

"Why do you want to talk to me?" the woman asks while looking around her as if she is checking no one is eavesdropping on our conversation. I almost don't want to talk to this woman anymore considering how eerie she is but I have to do my job, I can't disappoint Henry. If I lose this job, I may even have to move back home which is something that I am not ready to do at all.

"I think it's great to record what the neighbours think about her. It can be an important part of my research."

The woman thinks for a moment but then nods. "Alright, hen. Come with me. I'll answer all your questions."

Phew. I wasn't sure the woman would agree to an interview but I am glad she has. She starts walking and I follow her. This area is very calm and peaceful, very much in contrast with the city centre. Not many people are around and those who are are choosing to stay in their homes. I see a few people around on the way but I can tell they are tourists by the way they are dressed up. Lots of people who visit the Scottish Highlands make a stop here. It is a picturesque village and the loch nearby is quite popular among tourists. I can imagine this place gets crowded when the sun comes out. Today is not one of those days, which is why there aren't many tourists around. It's a dull, grey day today, the kind of day that would even make a normal human feel like a ghost.

The woman doesn't live too far, we are by her house within ten minutes. She takes me inside her house. "My sons are in school right now so I went out for a walk. Thank god I did. You don't want that witch to haunt you," she says as she closes the door behind me. The first thing I notice about her house is how messy and cluttered it is. There are all kinds of weird things on the walls and I don't recognise most things. I do see an evil eye pendant though, I recognise it because my mother has a similar one.

"No, I don't want anyone to haunt me." I hide my smile. Now that I am here inside the house, I feel uncomfortable. I now think it may have been a bad idea to just walk into a stranger's home. No one knows I am here. If this woman turns out to be a creepy murderer, no one would even find my dead body. It'd be easy to just kill me and throw my dead body in the loch. I take a deep breath and shake those thoughts away. I am strong enough to fight this frail woman, should it come to that.

"Would you like a cup of tea?" the woman asks but doesn't wait for an answer. She gets up and leaves before I can even say anything.

While she's away, something rubs against my leg. When I look down, it's a cat. A white cat almost as white as snow.

"Hello!" I say to the cat. The cat sniffs my hand and starts licking it.

"Oh, Snowy is here. He doesn't really like strangers usually," the woman says as she comes back with a cup on a saucer. I notice that she has come back with only one cup of tea. She places it in front of me. Snowy stops licking my hand and rests against my leg. He likes me more than Olive does. At least one cat likes me.

"I have a cat too. Her name is Olive and she is jet-black."

"Oh, dear. Why do you have a black cat? You know they're unlucky, right?" the woman says as she places a hand on her chest. I wasn't fond of her drivel anyway but now that she's coming for my cat, I particularly don't like her.

"I don't believe in such superstitions," I tell her and hope this would be the end of the topic. I take the cup in my hand but I don't drink it. I don't trust this woman at all.

"Well, it's not just a superstition. Although not all black cats are bad, they are just more susceptible to being used for dark magic. Perhaps the cat that you have is innocent, perhaps she is not," the woman continues droning on. I put the cup back on the table without drinking the tea. I take out my laptop. I want to be done talking to this woman as soon as possible.

"Can you tell me everything about the 'witch' that used to live, or as you say, still lives in that hut?" The woman's entire demeanour changes. While a few seconds away, she seemed like she was in control of her emotions, I can see that my question about the witch has shaken her.

While trembling in fear, she starts speaking, "My grandmother told me about her. Her name is Isabella, she was despised by all the neighbours around. We wanted her gone." She pauses and looks out the window. "She is a beautiful woman, I'll give her that. When you look at her, you can't tell she is an evil woman. She looks innocent, as if she can't even hurt a fly."

"You have seen her?" I look up from my laptop. I am making notes about everything that she says but I can't tell if all of this will be actually useful for my research.

"Oh, aye. When I was a child, some of my friends dared me to peek inside the hut. I didn't want to, but I did it anyway. I didn't see her at first, she somehow knew someone was looking at her so she hid behind the mirror. But then I did. She was hiding behind the mirror and she smiled at me, tempting me to open the door and free her. She could control me with her mind. Thankfully, my mother found me and took me away before I could free her."

I have to type really fast to write down each and every word. Once I am done, I look up at her. "Is it that easy to free her? Just open the door?"

"Open the door and break the vial, that's how you free her."

I cough and stop typing. "What vial?"

"That's how the priest captured her, he used the holy water and tied her spirit to the vial. If the vial breaks and the water seeps out, she is free to go wherever she wants." I delete everything that I have typed out so far. This woman is clearly a lunatic and not a word she says is useful to my research. Perhaps she saw me the other day and is now trying to scare me. Yes, that's a possibility.

"Thanks for letting me know, I think I should go now." I put my laptop back in my bag and start to get up. Snowy gets up too and scratches his paw against my leg.

"You can come and ask me any questions later if you want." The woman takes my hand and looks at me. "Take care of yourself, lass. You look very naïve to me."

I take my hand back and leave her house. What a waste of time that was. I wasted my time just talking to her. I go back to the hut and see there's no one around me. I take a few steps and open the door.

I am not going to believe in local tales and I am just going to do my job. As expected, there's no one inside. I even look behind the mirror and there is no one there. If the witch really was trapped in the hut, she has escaped already and there's nothing I can do about it now.

Even though I know that woman was lying, I don't feel very good inside the hut so I quickly take the box and leave before anyone can see me and accuse me of setting the witch free.

I take the box and go back to my office in Glasgow.

I show everyone the box. "You just stole the box?" Esme asks me.

"No, I didn't steal the box. It was just lying there in a stranded hut."

Henry shakes his head at me. "Either way, we can't keep the box with us. You have to submit it at the reception, it might be an important artefact." What? What was even the point of me getting the box if I can't even see the stuff inside?

"But, Henry, there are important things inside. They can be useful for our research."

"I am sure they are. But you have to submit it at the reception where they'll inspect the contents of the box. We can't just take the stuff we find. There's documentation involved. You may have harmed an important artefact or you've just stolen something from someone. Either way, you need to take it to the right people. Maybe you can see whatever is inside after they've done their work and write about it in your research report. But not now."

I somehow manage to hide my anger. "Alright, Henry. You can keep the box." I hand the box but he doesn't take it.

"Don't give it to me. You need to go to the Centre for Research Collection and submit it there. Explain what you did and they'll take it from you."

I take the box and go upstairs. I feel stupid for going so far just to get this box and I don't even get to peek inside. While I am in the lift, I open the box and find a diary. I take the diary out and keep it in my bag. There's no way I am going to give it to the university. I go to the receptionist and explain everything.

"Come back next week and I'll let you know if you can work with this or not," the bored-looking receptionist tells me.

I go back downstairs and do my research online. I would have loved to read whatever is written in the diary just now but I can't do it in front of everyone. I can only do it once I am back in my flat.

Meanwhile, I go back to the blog where I found Isabella's address to see if I can find something else. This blog is not a credible source so I can't use it in my research, but it's still interesting to read the articles posted here. I find the same local tale the woman I found in Luss told me about how Isabella is trapped in the hut.

I think about that woman's words again. Did I really set a witch free? No, how can that be? Although Olive did break the vial accidentally. The woman said that the witch will come to haunt me and force me to join her coven, but I am highly doubtful about that. Why would it be me? There's nothing special about me, I don't even think I believe in magic. I am just an ordinary girl, why would anyone invite me to be a part of their witchy group?

I find the blogger's email address in her 'Contact Me' section and I am tempted to send her an email. Her name is Courtney. Since she is so interested in witches, maybe she can tell me something.

Hi,

I am a researcher from the University of Glasgow, and I am writing a report on Isabella Gowdie. Since you have a section about her on your website, I thought you'd be interested in talking about her. Let me know if you're interested.

Warm Regards,
Kali

I press send and look at the screen. I hope she responds soon. I read about Isabella Gowdie some more online but there isn't enough information about her. The same information is repeated over and over again and I am guessing the source of this information is that occult blog. I really have chosen a difficult figure to write about.

I turn around to see what everyone's doing. All of them are hard at work. Henry is glaring at his screen, Esme is reading a fat book, Natacha is scribbling something in her notebook and Lisa is looking out the window as if she is thinking about something. I am wasting my time just sitting in the office. I could be back in my flat right now, reading Isabella's diary and doing some actual research.

I check the time, it's 3 p.m. I still have two more hours to go. I can't waste them just by sitting here.

"Hey, Henry. I need to go to the library to get a book. I am going to spend some time reading there if that's okay with you?"

"Oh yeah, sure. Go ahead." He doesn't even look away from his computer. I take my bag and leave.

Once I am in the library, I choose a secluded table on the third floor to work. The third floor is only for postgraduate research students and staff so there aren't many people here. Good, I can work peacefully. I sit by the window and take out Isabella's diary. It's covered in dust which I brush away with my hands.

10th September

I do not enjoy maintaining a diary but certain events have happened in my life that I must write down so I never forget they ever happened. I woke up this morning without an inkling that my life would change forever. I was out sitting in the garden perusing my book when Marianne called me. Her sister Annabeth is back in town and she wanted me to meet her. The last time I met Annabeth was when we were both much younger. Thus, when she came upon my door, I kept my book away and we both ran to her house.

I couldn't recognise Annabeth when I first saw her. Oh, how handsome she has grown up to be! She was dressed as a lady and when she saw me, she rushed to hug me. We were always best friends when we were little girls but when she went away to London, I thought she would forget about me but she hadn't! "Hello, Bella," *she said.* "You've turned into a beauty." *I blushed when she said that.*

I stayed with them for lunch and I noticed how Annabeth kept stealing glances at me. It was as if she wanted to tell me something but she couldn't in front of everyone. Marianne has invited me to join her for a morning walk tomorrow and Annabeth will be there too. Perhaps she will tell me then.

11th September
Annabeth and I visited the gardens today. Marianne didn't come with us so it was only just the two of us. After our walk in the gardens, we went to the museum. I am not fond of learning history at all but I went because I wanted to spend the day with Annabeth and learn all about her adventures in London. She didn't talk much about her life in London though. She was shaky and nervous as if something bad had happened there. She also told me she doesn't want to go back there. She wants to spend the rest of her life in Glasgow, marry a good man and live a simple life.

I turn a few pages and all the things written in Isabella's diary seem just as mundane. I didn't steal this diary to know what her friend is up to. I look up and see Henry walking towards me. I shut the diary and open another book as I see him coming towards me.

"It's 15 minutes past 5, what are you still doing here?" he asks. I check the time on my wristwatch, he is right.

"I didn't realise, I am going to go now."

"Kali, I was wondering if you'd like to visit the archives with me tomorrow. I found a few books that might help you."

"Sure, Henry."

"Cool. Bye." He turns around and leaves.

I read a few more pages of Isabella's diary on the train but it has been a disappointment so far. If she really was a witch, I expected her life to be more interesting. Her diary is very ordinary, it's something

I would have written in my younger years. There's no mention of anything occult.

I come back to my flat expecting Olive tearing apart another one of my beloved pillows, but it's awfully quiet when I return. She is not on my bed, and neither is she on the sofa. I look under my bed and she isn't there either.

"Olive," I shout. Olive never responded to me before either so I am not surprised when I don't hear anything, but I do get more upset. Where did she go?

I check all the windows and see that my kitchen window is open. I am so careless. I wear my jacket and head out to find my silly cat. Is this how she ran away from her previous owner too? Once I am out, I don't even know where she can be. I check the backyard and she is not there. Maybe she went out to play and got lost.

"Kali?"

I turn around and see Hans walking towards me with Olive in his arms. "Oh my god, Olive." I take her from Hans's arms and hug her. "Where did you go, you silly cat?"

"I found her in my backyard and recognised she was your cat. I took her in."

"Oh, thank you. I thought I lost her forever." I hug her and she tries to break free from my grip. I don't let her. When did I get so attached to her? I don't know but I can't bear the thought of losing her.

"You look a bit shaken, Kali. You want to come inside?" Hans asks me with a smile on his face which I find hard to say no to.

"Sure, Hans."

As soon as I am inside with Hans, Olive jumps from my arms and perches on his sofa attacking one of his pillows.

"God, I never knew cats are so annoying," I say and Hans laughs.

"They do have minds of their own. Have you never had a pet before?"

"I have a dog, Ruby. She lives with my mother in Birmingham. But I have never had a cat and Olive is very different from Ruby."

"You'll get used to them. They are nice creatures, sometimes annoying but nice most of the time." Olive looks up at me and blinks. The evil animal knows we are talking about her.

"Thank you again, Hans. I don't know how but I left my window open in the kitchen and she escaped."

"No problem, Kali. You don't have to keep thanking me. Thankfully, I was home today. I wasn't feeling well."

"Oh, no. What happened?"

"Nothing really." He takes a deep breath. "It's almost embarrassing when I say this but my fiancée and I broke up about three months ago, and I haven't been doing very well since then." I don't know what to say to this so I meekly smile. "I am sorry."

"It's alright. Anyway, there's a cat-friendly restaurant nearby where I was thinking of going for dinner. Would you like to join me?"

"Sure, let's go." Dinner with Hans? I am not going to let this opportunity go. Even if nothing romantic happens between us, I'd love to have a friend right now. As of now, I have no friends whatsoever apart from Olive. If I can even call her my friend. I'd love to have someone in my life, whether romantically or platonically.

The restaurant is a Mexican one, and when we reach there, it's quite busy. We have to wait for a while to get our table. I was expecting Olive to run around and make even more nuisance, but strangely she is really quiet and sits under my seat looking at everything that's happening around her.

"I sometimes feel bad about leaving her alone for the whole day, perhaps that's why she ran away today."

"Oh, don't be so hard on yourself." He smiles at me and my heart skips a beat. God, he's cute. Very, very cute.

"So, what do you do, Hans?" I just realise that I don't know anything about Hans. I find him cute but I am not going to properly fall for him until I know him better. I have learnt the hard way the perils of falling in love with someone too quickly after my experience with previous relationships.

"I am a lawyer. I only recently moved to Glasgow actually, I used to live in Madrid."

"Wow, that sounds fun." I have never been to Spain myself. While growing up, my parents never really went on holidays and most of my summers were boring. I've always been jealous of kids who did go on holidays.

"Yeah, not as much as you'd think. It was a lot of work, it's still a lot of work but I love my job." He pauses to change the topic. It seems he doesn't like talking about himself and would rather know more about me. I wonder if this is a red flag or not. "Mom was telling me you work at a university?"

"Oh, yeah. I am a researcher at the University of Glasgow." I try to keep my introduction short too. I don't want to blabber too much without knowing if Hans really is interested to know more about me or if he's just making polite conversation.

A waiter appears and we both order ourselves burritos.

"Would you like any drinks?" the waiter asks.

Hans looks at me. "You look like you need a glass of wine or two."

"Yes, please," I say while blushing. It's a weekday but well, I won't drink too much. A glass of red wine would be really nice right now.

Once we are served our food, Hans asks me, "What are you researching?"

"I am researching witches," I say and Hans's eyebrows rise in surprise.

"Oh wow, now that's a fun job. I wish I could learn hocus pocus all day at work."

I laugh. "It's not just hocus pocus, it's actually serious work. I have to read a lot of research papers and go through archives. Just the other day, I went to Luss to do some research, and I met this crazy old lady." I tell him about the entire incident and thankfully, he also finds it funny.

"Well, perhaps the woman was right and now you're being haunted," he says between mouthfuls. "Be careful at night, the witch might appear and try to steal your soul and lock it in a vial." He laughs.

"Oh, shut up, Hans." I also laugh. I feel more comfortable with Hans right now. I realise that I haven't spoken to someone at such length in a while. I do talk to Henry a lot but it's mostly work stuff. With Hans, it's banter. It feels good. I can see that Hans is more at ease too because he's now started talking more about himself.

"Do you use dating apps now that you're single?"

He puts the fork back on his plate and leans back in his chair. "I did download one just to see what's out there and my god, the dating scene is bleak right now."

"Really? What's the first message that you usually send to girls?" It's good to know that Hans is open to dating someone new. I am open to dating someone new too.

"Let's see." He takes out his phone and reads it to me, "Hey, my name's Hans and I'm 26 years old. I am university educated to a postgraduate level. I work full-time right now as a lawyer. In my spare time, I frequent the gym a fair and enjoy exploring new locations through travelling and definitely trying local cuisine! I'm 6'3 with light brown hair and hazel eyes with an athletic physique. Would love to chat to you and hopefully become friends! All the best, Hans." He puts his phone down. "So, what do you think?"

"That is the most boring introduction I've ever read in my life," I say while laughing.

"What? What is wrong with that? Wouldn't you be impressed by that?"

I shake my head to say no but I am not sure. "Who even mentions their height in their first message? Athletic physique? Seriously?"

"Well, if we men don't disclose our heights early on, you girls won't date us."

"That is not true at all!"

"That is very much true. Anyway, tell me about your love life," he says while taking a sip of his drink.

"My love life? To be brief: it sucks."

"A lovely girl like you shouldn't be having too much trouble with your love life." Lovely? He thinks I am lovely? I blush.

"You're stunning, you know that, right?" he answers my unspoken question.

"Thank you, you're very kind." It's been a long time since someone has complimented me and been genuine about it.

"So talk to me about the love life situation then. No one better to vent to than your neighbour," he says after ordering another round of drinks. I told myself that I was going to have one drink but I am enjoying this too much.

"Just annoyed about the whole thing really. I use dating apps and they don't work out for me very well."

"Damn. Maybe you should try dating one of your handsome neighbours?"

"My handsome neighbours? I think Mr Smith next door is quite handsome. He may be sixty years old but I am into dad bods."

He chuckles. "Oh, well I have a dad bod too. Don't you think? Anyway, what kind of dates do you like?" He pauses and then says with a wink, "Asking for a friend."

"I like walks, picnics, drinks, coffee. I am very adaptable when it comes to dates. Besides, dates are about the other person! If the person you're out with is boring, you won't enjoy anything." I take a sip of my drink. "What about you? When did you go on a date last time?"

"I like that a lot because I think variety is important, plus I promise I won't be boring." He winks. "As for your second question, probably about six months ago with my ex-fiancée. This is my first date since."

"This is a date?"

"We can make it a date if you want. What do you think?"

"I think I'd like this to be a date too."

Even though Hans is a new person in my life, I find him really easy to talk to. I don't even realise when the time goes by and it's time for me to go back home.

"I had a great time tonight, Kali," he says as we are walking towards home.

"Me too."

"Would you like to be friends with me on Facebook?"

"Sure." We both add each other. We walk together back home and Hans carries Olive in his arms.

"I hope I'll get to see you soon again," he says once we are at my door.

"Yes, we'll see each other soon."

Inside my room, I replay the date we had tonight. I look at Olive who is peacefully sleeping away on my pillow. The silly cat made me go on a date today. I know that woman said black cats are unlucky but I think the opposite is true for me. Olive has brought good luck to me. First, I found her around the same time I got a job and now a date. She is the harbinger of new things in my life. I plant a kiss on her forehead making her wake up from her slumber. She blinks at me and then goes back to sleep.

I am lying in my bed when I get a text on my phone. It's from Hans.

"Did you check under your bed? Olive might have let the witch inside." He follows it up with a laughing emoji. I know he's only joking but I check under my bed to make sure there is nothing under there. And there isn't. I feel silly for scaring myself like a child.

"There's nothing under there, I just checked. Stop scaring me!"

He responds with a laughing emoji and then a 'good night'. I respond back with an emoji and keep my phone away. Thoughts of Hans haunt me. I have a smile on my face but when I go to switch off my lamp, I can't bring myself to do it.

Even though Hans only said it is as a joke, I sleep with my lights on and keep Olive close by my side. I do not want any witch to come after me.

Chapter 3

Henry meets me at the office the next morning and takes me directly to the archives. The rest of our colleagues stay behind.

"Are you enjoying this job so far?" Henry asks me on the way. I take a moment to think about the question. Even though I wasn't enjoying this job as much in the beginning, I have grown to like it.

"Yeah, I am," I reply honestly. Apart from the fact that I might have set a witch free, yes, I am enjoying the job so far. The colleagues aren't too mean and the workload isn't too much. Henry, my boss is perhaps the best I have ever had in my life. I just got my first month's salary a few days ago and it is more than I need to enjoy my life and save for the future. What else could I want? I am even thinking of travelling somewhere on a long weekend. I may even buy a present for my mother to show her that I am not a complete failure in life.

Once we are in the archives, Henry gets me a few thick books. He puts them carefully on a pillow. "These are very important and old, be careful with them."

I nod to say yes. "What are these?" I ask.

"These are records from the Presbytery in Luss, the town where Isabella lived, they might be helpful to you."

"Oh, thanks. I'll start browsing them."

"Good. I have to look for a book for my own research so I'll be around. Just come to me if you need any help." Henry disappears amidst the bookshelves while I look at the thick book kept before me. It will take me the entire day to get through it. I look around me. There aren't very many people in the archives apart from me and Henry. It's so quiet here that I can even hear the sound of turning pages. I look at Henry who is sitting on the floor with his nose in another thick book.

I open the book kept before me and skim through it. The font is tiny and the pages are yellow. As I flip through them, there is dust on my fingers. Finding what I need to find is difficult in the book but after two hours of skimming through, I see Isabella's name on the page.

The Bewitching of Sir George Maxwell of Pollok

Mr George Maxwell of Pollok was an accomplished man. He obtained the honour of knighthood from King Charles II. Upon the fourteenth of October 1931, he was surprised in the nighttime with a fiery distemper and was fixed to the bed. The physician was called at the earliest and he abated the fiery heat but Sir George stayed in his bed for another eight weeks.

There had come to Pollok town, a young dumb girl named Isabella, seldom frequenting Sir George's house. A neighbour observed Isabella and reported that the girl had formed a wax picture with pins in his side, which was later found in her house upon investigation. It was deduced that the young woman had formed a pact with the devil and was using dark magic to entrap him in his love. The girl was also responsible for several murders in Luss. It was rumoured that she forced women to join their coven and when they said no, she killed them. The woman was put on trial by the priest and she finally confessed her sins. She refused to give the names of other witches in the coven. She cursed everyone present at her trial and their descendants, and for many years afterwards every tragedy in Luss was blamed on her curse.

Seriously? I blink at the page. The more I learn about Isabella, the more confused I get. She could make voodoo dolls? And actually curse people? That'd be pretty cool if she could do that. Who wouldn't want to be a witch if you get to do that? Hell, if I got the opportunity to curse people I don't like, I'd probably take it.

I copy down the passage on my laptop and get back to the book. I go through the rest of the book but Isabella isn't mentioned again. A few more hours pass and then it's time for the lunch break. I carefully shut the book and put it back where Henry found it. I won't be needing the book again, I have found what I needed to find.

"Did you find anything useful?" Henry asks during our lunch break. Henry and I take a late lunch break together and we go to an African wrap place nearby. I get myself a wrap with aubergine and halloumi and Henry gets the same.

"Henry, the more I learn about Isabella, the more I find myself getting confused. She is an astonishing figure, I'll give her that."

"Yes, she is. But don't worry too much, you don't have to find out everything about her within the first few months of your job. There is a reason why this project is a year-long."

"Yeah, and then my contract expires. I don't know what I'll do after that."

"Don't worry. We have several new research projects every year. The three other girls and I have worked before on them. I am sure you'll get hired again. You might even get to work with me again," he says and grabs my hand. I hesitate at first and then pull my hand away. He really needs to stop touching me all the time.

"What are you researching?" I ask Henry once I have finished my wrap. I have been so immersed in my own research, I have no idea what everyone else is doing. Henry does hold meetings time-to-time but they aren't frequent or long enough.

"Well, the witch I am researching about was just a regular woman. There are no instances of her doing anything. She was falsely accused by a jealous neighbour. Well, that's what it seems from what I've found so far."

"No voodoo doll?" I ask with my eyebrows raised.

"No. No voodoo dolls. Isabella is cooler, I guess. Imagine if she could actually do all that magic?" he says with a chuckle.

"What do you mean 'imagine'? I think she totally could do magic and she lives in that hut. Maybe I'll run into her at some point," I say sarcastically.

"Maybe she'll ask you to join her coven," Henry says with a laugh.

"Well, if she pays me more than this job does, you'll never see me again, Henry. I won't have to work 9-5 and I can just go around the forest making voodoo dolls. I am not turning down that opportunity."

I don't go back to the archives after lunch. I tell Henry I have to do some other work and he doesn't ask me any questions. I don't go back to the archives because I know I won't find anything else there. I have searched through the records book and there is no other mention of Isabella. I'd rather spend the rest of my day doing something other than reading old church records. I decide to take a walk around for a while before getting back to work. There is a beautiful park near the archives, a park so secluded and bushy, it's exactly what I need right now.

Reading through books and research papers isn't easy. My life has completely changed and so quickly. I am still struggling to get used to everything. A new job and potentially a new boyfriend? I am in a new city too. It's a lot of changes in a short amount of time. I know I asked for all these changes but it can still be overwhelming sometimes.

I go to the park and put some meditation music in my ears. Walks like these help me relax and help me clear my head. I have never been in this park so I get lost somewhere. I find myself in the middle of tall trees and have no way of getting out. I check my location on my phone but for some reason, it isn't working properly. I don't even have a signal on my phone. I take a few steps but I am somehow still surrounded by trees. I don't know how this happened.

"Kali?" I hear a voice calling my name but when I turn around, there's no one.

"Hello? Is anybody here?" I shout but I don't hear a response. I think if I heard a response, I'd be even more scared.

"Kali!" I hear someone call out my name again. I step towards the sound but suddenly, I am no longer surrounded by trees. I am back where I came from in the park. I check my phone again and now I have a signal and the GPS is working fine as well. Navigating the maps, I am able to bring myself out of the park. Once I am outside the gate, I turn around. The park is still secluded but I see someone in the distance. Someone standing exactly where I came from but I don't go back to find out who it is.

I go back to the office and I am a little disturbed by what just happened. I felt someone was following me the other day but I disregarded it thinking I was drunk. But again? Someone is following me. But who? I don't even know anyone in this city to have enemies. I did read about a kidnapping racket the other day. A group of men are kidnapping and raping girls. Could it be that? I am too stressed even thinking about this. But I don't have time to be stressed about this. I have to go back to work.

I get myself a cup of coffee and switch on my laptop.

"You okay?" Natacha asks.

"I am." I smile at her. It feels nice to have someone acknowledge my presence. It feels really lonely at work sometimes.

"You don't look okay."

"Nothing. I just went for a walk in the park and something happened to me." I narrate to her the entire incident. When I am done, it's not Natacha who responds but Esme. "That park is not a safe place. Loads of scammers walk about trying to rip people off. It could be one of them."

"Really?" This makes me feel a little bit better. I can fight off scammers. Yes, I can do that.

"Yeah, it's a ploy to scam tourists in the city. They sometimes ask you for money and sometimes they just snatch away your wallets. This is why I never go to that park alone. No one does."

"You're new to the city so you don't know much about it. But there are places where you shouldn't venture out alone," Natacha says.

"Well, I guess I am learning the hard way now."

"It's okay. We've all been there."

I turn back to my laptop when something strikes me. "But how did they find out my name?"

"Well, they could've been keeping an eye on you or something. I don't know," Esme says without looking away from her laptop.

I nod. I am not sure I am satisfied with the explanation but I don't press the matter further. The more I think about it, the more stressed I get. Besides, overthinking this issue won't help me further. I just have to be careful about where I am going and try not to go to secluded places alone. I guess this is one of the disadvantages of living alone, I don't have anyone to go to places with me. I didn't think of this before moving away from home. But so many girls around the world do this, they move away from home to seek a better life. I just have to be a little bit more careful, then I should be fine.

I pay the matter no more attention and turn back to my laptop. I see an unread email in my inbox from Courtney, the blogger I mailed the other day.

"Hey, Kali. I would love to answer any questions that you might have. Just call me." And then she leaves her number. This gets me excited. I wasn't expecting to hear back from her but now that I have, I am surprised by how willing she is to help me. I take my phone and walk out of the room to call her. She sent me this email just a few minutes ago. Maybe she might be available right now to take my phone call.

"Hey, this is Kali. I am the girl who sent you that email. I hope I haven't called you at a bad time."

"Oh no, not at all. I always love talking to new people who are interested in witchcraft." Her voice is high-pitched as if she is excited. She sounds very friendly and seems like someone who'd be able to help me a lot with my research.

To be honest, I am caught off-guard and I am not really sure where I should begin asking her about everything. There is silence over the phone before I rack my brain up and ask, "So, you really believe in the presence of witches? Do you think Isabella Gowdie is still alive?"

I hear her breathing on the other side before she speaks. "Isabella is one of the strongest witches to have ever existed in Scotland and the world. Her dead body was never found so people just assume that she is still alive. And yes, I do believe in witches. I can't believe you're asking me this question after reading my blog." She doesn't sound offended, just merely confused why I'd ask her this question in the first place.

"I am sorry, I didn't mean to offend you. I just wanted to confirm first. And I do know that Isabella's dead body was never found. But what really happened to her? Maybe she went somewhere and died there. Just because her body wasn't found where she was supposed to be doesn't mean her body wasn't found anywhere at all. Right?"

"A local priest trapped her in the hut for years so she could never escape. But people have peeked through the window before and they never saw her, dead or alive. If she died, her body should have been there. That is a mystery."

"I went to that hut," I tell her but I regret it instantly. This call was about me asking her questions, not me telling her about what I am doing.

"You what?" Her high-pitched voice is gone. She sounds surprised, almost shocked.

"I went to that hut and accidentally broke the vial."

"Oh, so that means you set her free." I am surprised by how calmly she says this and is not angry at me at all.

"You don't sound angry?"

"Why would I sound angry? As I said, Isabella is a strong witch, and we always knew she'd find a way to come back to us. You were just a medium."

"So is something bad going to happen to me now?" I can't believe I am asking this question, I can't believe I am actually taking all of this seriously.

"No, not at all. Why would Isabella hurt the person who set her free? She'd probably ask you to join the coven, in fact. You're lucky. You may have done what you did accidentally but you will be handsomely rewarded for it," she says matter-of-factly.

This is a lot of information for me to take in but I am simply ask, "What do witches do in a coven?"

"Magic. Spells. Seeing the future. Controlling minds. Taking revenge. Lots of things. But mostly, just living their lives the way they want to live. Most witches are harmless even though people don't really believe that."

"Oh." That is all I can manage to say. I don't even know what else to ask her now. This is a lot of information and I am still digesting it slowly.

"You don't seem too pleased. Trust me, Kali. What you have seen in movies and TV shows is rubbish. Witches don't hurt good people. Yes, Isabella has hurt people who tormented her in the past, but she never hurt good people. Trust me when I say this, you are very lucky. You're going to be really happy in life soon."

"You know a lot about this stuff and you seem to know so much about Isabella in particular, almost as if you know her personally. How did you get interested in her?"

"My grandmother was really fond of Isabella and she got me interested in all of this. You will find out everything soon since you'd be joining Isabella's coven any day now."

"I am not going to join any coven!" I am surprised she would suggest such a thing.

"You don't really have an option. You broke the vial and set her free. Whether you did it deliberately or not doesn't matter. You are already part of her coven in spirit. You just need to go through the initiation ritual now."

I do not want to discuss this topic so I ask about something useful. "Do you know anything else about Isabella?"

"Well, I don't. But you should talk to her granddaughter, she'd love to help you."

"Who's her granddaughter? Where does her granddaughter live? Where can I find her?"

"In Luss. I'll email you her contact details, she'd love to speak to you. And you'd find out more about Isabella and her coven from her. It's good that you're preparing for this." I am not preparing for anything, I am merely curious and working on my research. But I think explaining all of this to Courtney would be futile so I don't bother with it.

"Thanks, Courtney. You've helped me a lot. I'll contact you if I need any more help. Bye."

"Bye, Kali. Good luck with your journey to the coven."

***

I spend the rest of the day worried about whatever Courtney told me over the phone. She is convinced that I will join the coven now. I hate to say this but I don't think all of this is make-believe anymore. I have started to believe that at least some of it is true. Something is going on but I am not exactly sure what.

I am still deep in my thoughts when I get a call from Hans in the evening.

"Hey, Kali," he says in a chirpy voice when I pick up the phone.

"Hey, Hans," I try to match his tone but I am pretty sure I fail. Nonetheless, I am not sure I'd share any of this with him. We are still new and getting to know one another. I don't want him to think I am a crazy lunatic already.

"I am going to my Mum's tonight for dinner since she isn't feeling too well. She asked me to invite you too. Would you like to join us?" After the terrible day I've had, I would love to just be outside my house for a while. Talking to Courtney made my head hurt and being around other people would be more than welcome right now. I don't have to think for a moment before I know what I am going to answer.

"Sure, I'd love to, Hans." Hans's mom is lovely and I don't want to miss any opportunity to hang out with her. Besides, I am starting to feel scared of living alone now that people are making me believe that a witch is going to haunt me now. This is not good.

I always wanted to live by myself and now that I can finally afford to do that, I am starting to get scared. I do have a spare bedroom in my flat. It's only a single room but I am sure I'd be able to find a tenant. Maybe this would be a good idea. I won't be alone and I'd be able to get some extra cash. I convince myself that I'd be doing this for the extra money and not solely because I am starting to get scared of living alone. Olive would love some company too, perhaps. Or maybe she'd be unbothered by everything. She is very unpredictable when it comes to new people.

I get dressed up for the dinner. I was able to buy a few new dresses and I wear one of them tonight. I look at myself in the mirror. I look tired, not just physically but also mentally. I didn't expect this job to be so stressful before I began. I put some extra concealer on to hide the dark circles under my eyes.

Hans picks me up in half an hour and we both head to meet his mother. She only lives one subway station away from us so the journey isn't too long or tiring. Besides, it's good to see Hans. Being around him makes me forget all my problems.

"She lives nearby, why don't you live with your mother?" I ask Hans while we are in the subway.

"Alice used to live with me." I am assuming Alice is his fiancée. "I can go back and live with my mother but I am thirty now. I just don't want to live with my mother anymore." I nod. I didn't know Hans was thirty years old. He's almost eight years older than I am. Is that a big age gap? "What about you? Why do you live alone?" he asks.

"I am subletting someone's flat. She does have two bedrooms, and she gave me permission to find another flatmate if I want but I just didn't bother. But I am thinking of finding someone. It can get lonely sometimes." I don't tell him about what I am actually scared of. So far nothing has changed in my life so I shouldn't worry too much about being haunted right now but I still get scared sometimes. Thankfully, I have Olive with me even though she doesn't seem to like me very much.

"Don't worry, you can always hang out with me whenever you feel lonely," Hans says while putting his hand on my shoulder.

I rest my head against his shoulder and just smile silently.

"So nice to see you, Kali." Betty hugs me when she sees me instead of hugging her son first. "I am so glad you came." She lets both of us in. "You both are too early, I haven't even started cooking dinner yet," she says as she walks away to the kitchen.

"Mum, sit down. Don't bother, you're sick. We can order a takeaway."

"Yeah, Betty. We didn't come here to give you any more trouble. You must rest. Are you okay?" I ask.

Betty sits down on the sofa with us and waves her hand. "I am okay, Kali. I just had a little bit of fever, perfectly normal for women my age."

"I am going to go order some food while you girls chatter away." Hans takes out his phone and is busy ordering a takeaway.

"How is Olive?" Betty asks me as she puts one of her hands on my knees.

"She's doing great. She is quite an independent cat and lives alone for the most part of the day. It's quite fun to be around her. I don't have to do much to take care of her and she helps me feel not too lonely. I think it's a win-win situation for both of us."

"So, has she been truly abandoned? Did you try to find her owner again?"

"I think so. I check Facebook groups every day and I even talked to the local shelter, but no one has reported a missing cat. I think she has truly been abandoned but I just can't understand how anyone can do that to an animal, especially an animal as cute as Olive."

"People can be horrible, you don't know the things they do to innocent animals. Besides, Olive is a black cat. Loads of black cats get abandoned every year because of superstition. I am glad you are taking care of her now and don't believe in such rubbish."

"No, I definitely don't believe in any such thing. I don't think she can harm me in any way. In fact, I think she is taking care of me. I feel so much better knowing that she is with me every night."

"That's the magic of pets."

"I ordered some food. I hope you like it," Hans says as he puts his phone away.

The food is delivered swiftly while we are talking about our lives. Betty gets up to bring the cutlery but Hans makes her sit back down and gets up himself to bring the cutlery.

"You like Chinese food?" he asks me, handing me a plate of noodles and dumplings.

"I love Chinese food. I used to eat it almost every week while I was in Birmingham. There was this amazing Chinese food stall near our house and the food there was just delicious." That food place is the only thing I miss about Birmingham, nothing else. In fact, I am trying to forget everything about my life there.

"Why did you move all the way up here, Kali?" Hans asks.

I shrug. "I needed to move away from Birmingham at some point, I couldn't stay there for my whole life. I had heard so many great things about Scotland, so I packed my whole life and moved here. I don't regret it." I don't want to get into details just yet. Not in front of Betty. It's better to keep some things secret.

Hans smiles at me. "Aye, there's something about Scotland. Have you explored the country much yet?"

"No, I haven't. I haven't even explored Glasgow properly yet. Just some shopping centres in the city centre and that restaurant you took me to last time. Oh, and I have been to Luss for work, but that's about it."

Betty turns to Hans. "You must show her Scotland."

"I'd love to. You should come to the Isle of Skye with me. I am going there with some of my pals at the end of the month, there's a spot for one more in the car."

I think about it. It fits perfectly well with my plan of going somewhere away for the weekend now that I have money to do things. "Sure, I'd love to." So it's decided then. I'll go to the Isle of Skye at the end of this month.

We spend the rest of the night talking about anything and everything. It's good because I am not stressed anymore. Hans and I come back home late at night with our bellies full. "I think I overate," I tell him while suppressing a burp.

"Don't blame yourself, the food was too delicious. You want to come inside and have a glass of wine?" Hans asks while pointing to his flat.

"Don't tempt me, Hans. Tomorrow's a Wednesday and I have to wake up early. Maybe we can do something on Friday?"

"Sounds good, I'll see you then."

I come back inside my flat and lie down on my bed. Olive jumps on me and scratches my sweater. "I am sorry, Olive. I leave you alone for such long periods of time, I feel horrible." I plant a kiss on top of her forehead. She snuggles up to me and I hear her snoring softly. I fall asleep too.

The next morning I wake up to find my kitchen dirty. There are broken eggs on the floor, the juice is spilt everywhere and my vegetables are in the trash can. Oh my god, Olive is so naughty. Did she do this because I left her alone last night?

I find her perched on my bed and scold her. "Olive, that's bad." I don't think she understands me because she continues looking at me without blinking. I sigh. She's too cute and I can't bring myself to be angry at her for too long. I clean my kitchen and quickly take a shower. There is nothing left for me to eat, and I don't have time to go to the grocery store and then cook myself something. I have to leave for work on an empty stomach.

I get myself a huge cup of coffee once I am in the office. Only Natacha is on her computer, everyone else is not here yet. I sit at my table sipping my coffee with my head in my hands.

"You okay, Kali?" Natacha asks and I look up. I hate that people can tell I am not okay in the office.

"Just a rough morning. My cat destroyed my kitchen this morning because I left her alone last night."

She laughs, and her laugh makes me laugh too. "What a silly cat."

"I know, first-world problems. How's your research going?" I ask her.

"Meh. Some days are good, some are not. I think your witch is the most interesting one since she was alive until the last century and you get to do field research. The rest of us are stuck with these boring research papers." Oh, if only she knew I might have accidentally set my witch free. I'd have a way bigger problem than just having to read boring old research papers. "Did you find anything interesting?" she asks.

I am not sure how much I should tell Natacha. She's my colleague so I should be able to discuss everything with her but I am not too sure. "Well, apparently Isabella's body was never found and some people believe that she's still out there looking to recruit witches for her coven." I laugh, but Natacha doesn't laugh with me. "What? You don't find this bizarre and funny?" I ask her.

"You know, I find all these covens really interesting," she says while leaning back in her chair.

"I haven't found much about her coven so far, or any coven at all. I don't think I even completely understand covens." This piques Natacha's interest and she gets up to come sit next to me.

"Basically, witches used to practise in groups of thirteen. Practising in groups makes their witchcraft stronger. Geilis, the witch I am focusing on, was the leader of her coven. She was trying to find twelve women so that she could help in the Jacobite Rebellion. Do you know why Isabella was trying to recruit the rest of the witches?"

"I... I don't know. I never thought about that." Now I feel silly that it never occurred to me that I should find out about Isabella's coven if I can't find much information about her.

"You must try to find out about it. Every coven had a motive. I am sure Isabella's coven must have had one too."

I nod, I am completely lost in my thoughts. Natacha has given me a lot to think about.

"Hey, girls." Henry comes with a big stack of books in his hands and interrupts our conversation.

"Hey, Henry," we both say in unison.

"You know, we all should share our research with each other. Like I helped you learn about covens, maybe there is something in your research that can help me," Natacha tells me as she's walking back to her computer.

I nod and get back to my work. She's absolutely right. And now she's given me a lot to think about. I begin my research on covens and I am busy reading a research paper on witchcraft when I get a call from an unknown number. I hang up, I don't want to speak to anyone right now, but whoever is calling me is persistent. When they call me the third time, I pick up the phone.

"Hello, who is this?" I try to hide my annoyance but fail miserably.

"Hello, am I speaking to Kali?" a woman asks me nervously.

"Uh. Yeah. Who are you?"

"I am Jenna, Isabella Gowdie's granddaughter. Courtney gave me your number." I look around the office and leave. I can't be having this conversation in front of everyone.

"Hey, hi," I say once I am outside.

"I am sorry I called you out of the blue. Courtney told me about you, about your visit to my grandmother's hut, and I have been waiting for your call since then."

Courtney gave me Jenna's contact details the other day, but I never bothered to call her. I was too creeped out by our conversation. And I was still preparing my questionnaire for the interview with her. She must have given Jenna my contact details too. "I am sorry, I just got busy with all the work. I am doing a research report on your grandmother."

"I know, Courtney told me. I was wondering if you'd like to meet me sometime?"

"Where do you live, Jenna?" Meeting her would be better rather than having a phone interview. It would be a good opportunity to find out more about Isabella and her coven.

"I live in Luss, but I am in Glasgow right now. Would you be able to meet me today?"

I look around me. Surely meeting Jenna is more important than reading any essay. "Sure, Jenna. Let's meet outside the West End subway station in two hours. Does this work for you?" She responds in the affirmative.

I go back inside the office and tell Henry about Jenna. "She is the granddaughter of Isabella Gowdie, so I am sure she'll be helpful."

Henry almost jumps in his seat with excitement. "Oh my god, Kali. That's a great source." I look around the room and almost everyone is impressed with me and perhaps even jealous. No one else is getting to do actual field research interviews, it's just me. My research is way more interesting than theirs and everyone knows that.

I find Jenna outside the subway station and recognise her even though I have never seen her before. She looks very much like her grandmother. The high cheekbones and thin lips. It's almost as if someone has made a photocopy of Isabella.

"Hey, Jenna."

"Hey, Kali." Her voice is high pitched as if she is both nervous and excited about the meeting. I take her to a cafe nearby, which is usually busy with students. I order two cappuccinos. Before leaving, Henry told me it's usually the interviewer who is expected to pay for the expenses but thankfully I'd be able to claim them from the department.

"So, what was your grandmother like?" I ask once our coffees are served. I left my questionnaire behind in the office. It's better to just go with the flow and get as much information from her as possible.

Jenna's face lights up like a Christmas tree. "She is the bravest woman I know. I want to be as great as her someday." I notice that she is using the present tense to describe her.

I cough. "I am glad you like your grandmother so much, did you spend a lot of time with her as a child?"

"Oh, no. I never met her, I only heard stories about her from my mother before she passed away."

"Oh, I am sorry." I shift uncomfortably in my chair.

"Don't worry, she died when I was barely ten years old. My aunt adopted me and raised me."

"So, if you've never met your grandmother, how do you know she was so cool?" I ask.

"Well, did you know that she was romantically interested in her friend?"

"What?" I cough while taking a sip of my hot coffee.

"Yeah, that's something that people try to hide about her. Even my aunt tried to hide it, but she eventually told me. I didn't understand what it meant when I was a child, I only understood it when I grew up."

"Oh." I have to admit that I am shocked. And then I think back to her diary and her friend Annabeth. Her diary makes sense now. She has written a lot of pages on Annabeth.

"Yeah, I was shocked too. This is one of the reasons why she is called a witch by everyone. Because she refused to conform to the ideals of society. People found out about her and how she felt for her friend. It was her friend's mother who suspected it and then her suspicions were confirmed when she read Isabella's diary. Isabella loved her friend but she was betrayed by her. What happened to her was very tragic." I know what Jenna is talking about. Isabella mentioned something about it in her diary but I can't recall it right now.

"You're talking about Annabeth?" I ask.

"How do you know her name?" This time it's she who is shocked and coughs up her coffee.

"I found her diary in her hut."

Jenna nods. "Yes, you must have. She had a habit of keeping several diaries. Did you find all of them?"

"There was more than one?" How did this not occur to me before? There should have been more than one diary. But where could they be?

"Of course, her life couldn't fit in just one notebook." It does make sense when she says that. The diary that I found was thin and incomplete. There must be more somewhere. But where?

"But there weren't any others in her hut. I only found one, it was kept in a large box along with the vial. I searched the hut thoroughly and didn't find anything else."

"Someone must have taken the rest of them away. Maybe the priest who trapped her," she says while shrugging her shoulders. Now where would I find this priest? Is he even alive?

"Yeah, maybe," I mumble.

We drink our coffees in silence as we both try to digest this information. "Jenna, do you know anything about Isabella's coven?"

"No, my mother or aunt never told me about that."

"Oh." It's hard to hide the disappointment in my voice. "Jenna, you said that your grandmother was in love with her friend, but she must have been married to a man if she gave birth to your mother. Why don't you tell me something about him?"

"I don't know anything about my grandfather and neither did my mother. I think he left her really early in life."

I nod. I chat with Jenna for a while, but she doesn't have any more important information for me. Although she does seem mesmerised by me as if she is meeting a local celebrity.

"Jenna, I am really curious. Why did you want to meet me so desperately?"

"Because if what I've heard is true, then you are the next witch of her coven. I always wanted to be a part of the coven but I know I am not good enough. But there must be something about you. You seem special."

"What? What are you talking about, Jenna?" She's saying the same thing Courtney said to me. They both think that I am a witch now but nothing magical has ever happened to me. I am the most ordinary girl there can ever be.

"My grandmother Isabella was looking for the thirteenth witch to join her coven before she was acquitted as a criminal. Since you've set her free, you've already begun your journey of becoming a witch in a way."

"Jenna, I am not a witch. I am just an ordinary girl who is doing her job to pay her bills."

"Kali, don't you realise?" she asks while putting her cup of coffee with a little too much force. She seems a little annoyed, even angry at me. As if she's explaining something to a toddler who refuses to learn.

"Realise what, Jenna?" I put my cup down too.

"There's no way out for you now. You are going to become a witch, whether you like it or not."

Chapter 4

In the evening, I have to go to Tesco before getting on the subway since I have no groceries left. I need to find a cat trainer if Olive continues doing this. I always thought dogs were the naughty ones, but I guess Olive is just as notorious too.

I am filling my basket with all kinds of food items when my phone rings. It's my mother. I haven't spoken to my mother since I've come to Glasgow. One of the reasons why I left home in the first place is because I didn't want to be around her anymore. What does she want right now?

"Hey, Mom." I fake as much enthusiasm as I can. Even though I don't like her and maintain my distance from her, I'd still like to be cordial. She's my mother after all, whether I like it or not.

"Hello, Kali. Where are you?" That's how my mom really is. Her first question to me isn't how I have been or how I have been settling in a new city. It's where I am.

"I am in Tesco."

"Hm, what are you buying in Tesco?" What else would I buy in a grocery store besides groceries? I have to compose myself before responding or else I might lash out at her. Even when she doesn't say something annoying, I get easily annoyed by her and then it'd be difficult for me to be polite.

"I am buying some cup noodles I can eat for dinner tonight."

"Cup noodles? Is that all you've been eating lately? You must have got fat. Cup noodles aren't very healthy. You must get some vegetables and fruits." And my mother begins saying things I don't want to hear. Things that I've tried to ignore throughout my life. For my mother, I've always been fat, ugly and a complete failure in life. No matter what I do, she always finds faults in me. I'll never be good enough for her and I've made my peace with that. I can't change her but I can ignore her.

"Okay, I will." That's all I say. There's no point in telling her that I'd rather not talk about my weight right now. I am so ready to hang up on her.

"And make sure you buy enough groceries for two," she says before I can hang up.

"For two?" This can only mean one thing and if it is what I think it is, I am almost ready to cry.

"Yes, I am coming over." I drop the toilet paper rolls I have in my hands. I don't want her to come over. I want to be away from her.

"You're coming over? When? Why?"

"Why? Does a mother need a reason to visit her daughter?"

"I guess not," I mumble.

"I am on the train right now, I will be at the Glasgow Central station in about fifteen minutes. Can you pick me up?"

"You're reaching in fifteen minutes and you're just calling me to let me know?" This is so typical of my mother. Now I wish I hadn't picked up my phone in the first place.

"Darling, if I had told you before that I am coming over, you would have made some excuse. I know how much you lie." I think I am starting to get a headache.

"I'll pick you up," I say, because I know I have no other option and hang up the phone. There's no point in debating anymore if she's already here. I check my time, it will take me about fifteen minutes to reach there. I quickly pay for my things and head out.

My mother is already at the station when I reach there. I see her with a giant suitcase standing amidst the crowd looking for me. The size of the suitcase tells me she is going to stay with me for a while. I do not look forward to it.

"Hi, Mom." I fake a smile and she forcefully hugs me.

"I have been waiting for you for so long. Where were you?" She is clearly lying since her train must have reached here barely a few minutes ago.

"I was on my way, if you had told me you were coming, I would have reached on time."

"I have only just reached here and you're already starting to get mad at me. Why do you hate me so much, Kali?" In this moment, I want to punch my mother, which isn't a very nice thing to do, but my mother just brings out the worst in me.

While I usually take the subway, I call a cab today so that we can comfortably reach my flat. My mother's big suitcase would be a pain to carry on public transport and I know that she'd expect me to carry it. Why does she have such a ginormous suitcase with her in the first place? I try to remember if my flat is clean. I hope it is, otherwise my mom would just find another thing to get on my nerves.

"This is not a very pretty city, Kali. Why'd you move here?" my mother asks while we are in the cab. I look at the driver who is clearly a Glaswegian, and I hope he is not offended.

"It's a fun city, Mom. You've just arrived, you'll see. I will show you around." I don't know why I am always rushing to please my mother when I know that I don't like her at all. I don't want to show her around, I don't even want to be around her but here I am acting like the perfect daughter.

Once we have reached home, she looks around the neighbourhood as the driver and I struggle to lift her heavy suitcase. "Quite an ugly neighbourhood," she says. The driver looks at me as if he is trying to tell me what a crackhead my mother is.

I am thankful I live on the ground floor so I don't have to take her heavy suitcase upstairs. Once we are inside and I have given her a glass of water, I calm down a little. I can do this. She is my mother. I have lived with her my whole life. I can bear her presence for a few more days.

"So, how have you been?" I ask my mother since she hasn't asked about me so far.

"I am alright, Greg and I are doing great. But he's gone away for a week so I decided to visit my daughter." Greg is my mother's new boyfriend who I despise. He is only five years older than me and mentally, he seems to be five years old. I have no idea what he sees in my mother, but at least he keeps my mother distracted and she doesn't disturb my life too much.

"How long are you going to stay?" I ask without meeting her stare.

"I haven't decided yet. Maybe a week, maybe a month. Greg and I are going to Oban after this, so whenever Greg is free from his work in Manchester, I'll leave."

"So you just decided to come here? Why didn't you come when Greg was not at work?" It's a genuine question but I can see that it has offended my mother.

"Because my dear little daughter, I wanted to see what you're up to. You decided to leave your poor mother behind without a thought. You don't care about me but I do. I wanted to see your new life. You may not like me but I still love you." Love. This is the word she uses to get things from me. I have fallen for it many times in my life but it doesn't have the same effect on me as it used to. She has never loved me and she never will. I hope Greg comes soon. I can handle her for a week, but for a month? No chance.

Olive walks into the living room and my mother screams.

"What is that?" she asks with a disgusted expression on her face as if she has just stepped on shit while wearing her newest, most expensive shoes.

My mother's scream scares Olive, and she hides under the table. I get up and take her in my arms. "Olive, meet my mother. Mom, this is Olive."

There is a silence around the house where no one knows what to say. A moment passes before my mother says, "You have a cat in your house? A black one? Black cats are evil, Kali. They bring bad luck. You must throw her out of this flat right now." Of course, she'd say something like this. I should have been prepared for this the moment she told me she was coming over. Growing up, my mother used to believe in the strangest things. She believed cutting my nails at night would bring bad luck and I was prohibited from eating meat on Tuesdays. When I asked for the logic behind these things, she told me that this is how our ancestors have always done things and I should follow in their footsteps. I tolerated these things while growing up because I didn't have any other option. But I am an adult now who earns her own money and lives in her own place. Her rules won't work here.

"Mom, Olive is not going anywhere. She was abandoned by her previous owner, I am not going to do the same to her," I tell her. If I have to choose between the woman who gave birth to me and the cat that I found a few days ago, I'd pick my cat without a doubt.

"Then have her put down. There are too many cats in the world, one less cat in the world wouldn't make much difference," she says and my jaw drops. Imagine suggesting an innocent animal is murdered simply because you believe it's unlucky for you. Such heights of narcissism.

I kiss Olive's head and this seems to scare my mother even more. "I am not going to do any such thing. She is not evil, nor is she going to bring me any bad luck. This is my flat, not yours. Your rules don't apply here."

My mother looks at me as if I just stabbed her. "Okay, you have grown up now. You can do as you please."

I shrug. Of course, I am going to do as I please, I won't need her permission for that. I take her suitcase and put it in the smaller bedroom. "Mom, you can sleep here."

She looks into her bedroom and then into mine. "Why do I get the smaller bedroom? The bed here is too small."

"It's a single bed, big enough for you. And I already live in the bigger bedroom. It would be too inconvenient for me to shift my stuff just for a few days." She doesn't seem too pleased with this, but thankfully doesn't continue to bicker. I leave her for a moment when she disappears into her room. She comes out a moment later with a towel in her hand.

"Where's the bathroom?" she asks. I show her the way as well as the kitchen.

"You can use everything here but please be mindful that I have only sublet this flat and I need to leave everything as it is when I leave."

This was an innocent suggestion but it has angered her. "What do you think of me, Kali? I am not going to go about your flat destroying things. I raised you by myself as a single mother over the years, I know how to live in a house without burning it down."

"I didn't mean that," I say but it has no effect on her. She bangs the bathroom door shut in my face. I go back to my bedroom and scream into my pillow. I do not want her here and I need to find a way to get rid of her soon. I was stupid to think that I could tolerate her. I can't. Nothing has changed in the way she treats me and nothing ever will.

My mother has always thought of her as a victim. She thinks the universe has treated her awfully and the whole world owes her an apology. The truth is that my mother is somewhat correct. She has gone through a lot in her life. My father didn't treat her well and neither did her parents. And for some reason, she believed that it's all because of me. I must have done something for my dad to treat her poorly. She may not say it, but she wants me to apologise for my dad with my actions. I just don't see why I should do it.

She comes out of the bathroom in about an hour and seems to be in a better mood now. She's wearing one of my old T-shirts but I don't say anything. I never liked that T-shirt anyway. She's unpacking her suitcase in her room when I knock on the door.

"What do you want to eat for dinner? I can make some rice for you and we can eat it with the leftover Thai curry I ordered last night," I ask.

She looks up as she is putting her clothes in the drawer. "You're going to feed your mother some stale old curry? I expected better from you. Is this how you live?"

I actually live worse than this. I regularly eat out-of-date food but I am yet to get food poisoning. Of course, I don't tell her that. I sigh. "I can cook something fresh for you. Tell me what you want to eat."

She gets up and goes into the kitchen to take a look at the things I've kept in my fridge. Usually my fridge is empty but thanks to my Tesco shopping earlier in the evening, I have most of the basic things one needs to eat in my fridge.

My mother turns around and smiles sweetly at me. "Why don't you go relax? I'll cook something for both of us."

"Okay." This is the first nice thing my mother has said to me all evening. I leave her alone in the kitchen to play with Olive, who is clearly disturbed by my mother's presence. She is hiding under my blanket. I lift the blanket up and cuddle her. "Don't worry, Olive. It's only for a few days." I am not sure if I am saying this to reassure Olive or myself. And I don't even know if my mother will be around for just a few days or more than that.

I am trying to assure Olive while watching Netflix when my mother opens my door. I wish she'd knocked on my door instead but then my mother has never knocked on my door before coming in while I was growing up, why would she suddenly change and do it now? In order to avoid another fight, I let it go.

"Dinner's ready!" she says.

I go into the kitchen to see what she's cooked for dinner. My mother is a very unpleasant person, but if there's one thing she's good at, it's her cooking. She has made an eggplant curry that she serves with rice and a side salad. I help my mother serve dinner and we both sit together to eat. I try to remember when was the last time we sat together and ate. I can't remember it, it must have been ages ago.

I stayed at home during uni to save rent money but even while we were living together, we did our best to avoid each other. I did it on purpose and she did it because she was busy doing her own thing, which mostly included gossiping with neighbours and browsing our local charity shops. She never bought anything and yet she went out everyday. Eating dinner together was never our thing. I tried to spend my nights with my friends or whichever boy I was dating. And when I was home, I often ate pot noodles or microwave meals in my room.

Eating dinner together with someone close to you is such a simple thing but it's something I've always enjoyed. It feels so intimate. I put a spoonful of rice with curry in my mouth. It's absolutely delicious. My mother never cooked much for me but I remember whenever she did, it was heavenly. Just like it is now.

"The food is delicious, Mom. Thanks for making dinner." I smile at her and she smiles back at me.

"While I am here, I'll cook for you everyday. I can't let my daughter eat pot noodles every night, can I?"

Perhaps it won't be so bad living with my mother.

***

"Kali, wake up!" My mother is standing by my bed with a cup of coffee in her hand. I check the time. It's 5:30 am!

"Why did you wake me up so early? I leave for work at 8:30." I look outside my window, it's still dark outside. The days are starting to get shorter as winter is around the corner. I look at my mother and she is wearing a bright pink hoodie along with purple leggings. She also has a headband which looks way too small for her head.

"Waking up early is good for you. You should wake up early every day and workout. Perhaps you can go for a walk? It will help you lose weight. Maybe we should go together. Is there any park nearby?" Her voice is so high-pitched, it scratches my ear as if I have put a nail in my ear.

"I am not in the mood to go for a walk. You can go by yourself. There's a park called Elder Park right around the corner," I say and cover my head with my blanket before she can say anything further.

"Alright," she says and thankfully leaves. I hear her banging my room's door and then the main door too loud for this time of the day. I peek outside my blanket to make sure she is away. Olive, who was hiding under my blanket while my mother was here, takes her head out too and looks at me. "She won't be here for too long, Olive. I promise."

I try to go back to sleep for another hour and a half, but now that I am awake, I struggle. After tossing and turning for twenty minutes and annoying Olive, I get up. I decide to use the extra time that I have to cook a fancy breakfast for myself and my mother. I want to thank her for dinner last night. Although I don't know why I am always trying to impress her, she would never like me no matter what I do. I never realised that mothers are capable of hating their children to this extent, but oh well.

Since even Olive got annoyed by my mother, I give her the special cat food that I bought only for special occasions. She really likes it, and I hope she'll be in a better mood. For myself and my mother, I am going to make French toast, beans and sausages. A proper English breakfast. My mother always liked that.

I get the eggs out of the fridge and break them with a fork, but instead of egg yolk, blood comes out of it. I almost puke at the sight of it and throw it away. I break another one and once again there's blood. I take another one and another one and all of them are the same. I take the last egg from the box hoping at least this won't disappoint me, but when I break it, a half-formed chick dipped in blood comes out.

This has never happened to me before. I take all of the broken eggs and throw them in the dustbin. I have a sudden urge to puke after looking at all this mess and I can't stop myself. I puke my guts out in the bathroom. Once I am done, I am no longer hungry. I scrap the idea of making a proper breakfast and clean my kitchen instead. By this time, my mother returns.

"What are you making?" she asks.

"Uh, just cereal and milk."

"I knew you'd get lazy when you move away, you should be eating proper food. Not this dry cereal." She opens my fridge. "You don't even have eggs, how careless you are! Did you purposely not buy them because you knew I like them so much?" It takes all my strength to not roll my eyes in front of my mother.

"I'll bring some in the evening, Mom."

"Where's your cat? She's not in the living room?"

"No, she's in bed. She doesn't wake up this early," I say while I pour some cereal in two bowls, one for her and one for me. She takes the chair next to me and looks at me in confusion.

"You let that dirty cat sleep in your bed?" she says before she takes a spoonful of cereal in her mouth.

"Her name is Olive, and she is not dirty. She actually helps me sleep better every night. And it's my bed, not yours. You don't have to worry about it, Mom."

She puts her hand on her chest. "All cats are dirty. You should be especially wary of the black ones. They lure spirits into your house. You don't want to be murdered by some dark spirit, do you?"

"Mom, please leave Olive alone. She's just an innocent cat."

"What if she gets into my bed? What if she lures something evil into my life?" She has her hand on her chest as if having a cat in the same house as her is the most tragic thing that has happened to her ever.

"She won't do that," I say even though I am dreadfully sure she'd do that. She'd purposely get into my mother's bed if she knows how much that would bother my mother.

"I am going to put a lock on my door, just in case. Where did you even find this cat? I never knew you were fond of cats."

"Someone abandoned her and she was outside my door. I just couldn't leave her outside."

"Kali! Are you telling me that you don't even know where this cat has come from?" she screeches in my ear and I simply shrug. "Do you know how dangerous that is? Someone could have put her to do this. Someone could have purposely left her outside your house. This could be a scheme."

"Mom, are you serious? Olive doesn't follow anyone's orders. Do you seriously think she came to mess my life up because someone is making her do this?"

"That could happen. You can never be sure with black cats. Think about it, Kali. Are you sure you want to keep this dirty, strange black cat inside your home?"

I leave my bowl of cereal on the table as my response. I am no longer hungry. And I no longer want to hear my mother objecting to everything that is happening in my life. "I am getting late," I tell my mother and leave her slurping her bowl of milk in the kitchen.

I take a shower and get dressed. Before I am about to leave, I tell my mother, "Olive usually just chills around the house when I am gone. Can you promise me you won't be mean to her when I am away?"

"Why would I be mean to that dirty cat? Besides, I have my own plans. I am going to go out in the city to meet some friends," she says while disappearing into her bedroom. I follow her.

"I didn't know you have friends in Glasgow." She has been here barely twelve hours and she has friends? As far as I know, Mum has never travelled up north nor did she have any friends who live here. None that I know of. It's not just me who's been starting a new life, Mum has been doing new things too. I am glad that she has other passions in life besides disliking me.

"You don't know many things about me, you never spend time with me to know. If you had called me, I would have told you about all the new hobbies I have been into since you left."

Instead of bickering, I leave her and kiss Olive goodbye. I hope my mother won't annoy her too much. And if she does, I hope Olive uses her long talons that she isn't shy to use on me.

The subway is more crowded than usual. I don't get a seat and I have to stand throughout the journey. I put my earphones in when I see someone familiar in the crowd. I look again, but they disappear. I thought it was Isabella for a moment, but how could it be? Perhaps it was Jenna. I look again, but the crowd blocks my view and there's no way to make sure. The crowd doesn't thin until my station and then it's too late to find out who it was. I pay it no mind and continue walking towards my office.

"Hey, Henry." I am the last one to reach the office today, thanks to my mother. Everyone is sitting around a round table with one vacant chair that I presume is for me.

"Hey, we were just waiting for you. Come, we are having a group discussion." I take my coat off and join their table. Henry continues, "So, I was just talking to Dr Philip Gregory, he is the Dean of the Scottish History department and he was telling me there is a two-day conference next month and at the last moment, a research team pulled out due to technical issues. He suggested we all take the spot and talk about what we have researched so far. What do you guys think?"

"Do we all have to present?" Esme asks what I have on my mind. Public speaking is not something I am comfortable with. Besides, I don't know if I have enough research to talk about in a conference. My research is too fractured and I need more time to make it cohesive.

"Well, it's a twenty-minute spot. There's five of us and I was thinking that I could do the introduction and then each of us can speak for maybe three-four minutes? It's not a lot and we won't have to prepare that much."

"But what are we going to present? We don't have a lot of data to present," Natacha says, and all of us nod our heads to show agreement.

"We don't have to do an extensive presentation. I'll do the introduction where I talk about how innocent women were called witches for things they didn't do. Then all of you can give examples and talk about the witch you are doing your research on. Not a lot, just a few lines." Lisa is the only one who says 'sure' while the three of us say nothing. "How about you, Kali? What do you think of this?"

"I—I don't know, Henry. I have never presented my research like that. Public speaking makes me nervous." He takes my hand and holds it in front of everyone. "We all have to present our research at the end of the year, I think this would be a good practice session." I pull my hand away instantly. Why does he have to be so touchy? It's inappropriate and so unprofessional. I wonder if Henry can figure out that him touching me all the time makes me uncomfortable.

"Alright, I am in," I say, hoping he won't hold me again. Three four lines on Isabella Gowdie? I think I can manage that. Public speaking is something I've never done before in my life. It makes me nervous. But I know that I am in a new phase of life and in this new phase, I'd like to try new things, things like public speaking.

"I am in, too," Natacha says. So do Lisa and Esme.

"That's great, girls. This would be fun, I assure you. If the History Department likes what we have done so far, they might increase our funding. We'd be able to work on this project for longer." Henry and Lisa are the only ones who are excited. The rest of Esme, Natacha and I are nervous and it's very apparent on our faces. I am glad I am not the only one.

"Henry, do we get to read from a paper or do we have to memorise our lines?" Natacha asks a very important question. My memory isn't bad so I'd be able to remember a few lines but nervousness makes me forget things and I may forget everything I learn as soon as I get on stage.

"I think it would be better if we all memorise and speak rather than reading it from a paper. That would be more impressive." Memorising a few lines won't be difficult, I just hope I don't forget them as soon as I am in front of people. "So, I would suggest we prepare our outlines and then practise on Monday. Does that sound good?"

All of us murmur a shaky yes. "Good. Let's get to work." I am about to leave when Henry asks me to stay behind as other girls go back to their computers. "How did it go with Jenna?"

"It went great, I found out about Isabella's missing husband and the fact that she was romantically interested in her friend. It all sounds like a really interesting novel."

"What?" Henry is understandably shocked. Anyone would be. Isabella is more interesting than any of us ever thought she'd be. I won't lie, the fact that I am doing my research work on her makes me want to come to the office every day. It's much better than a monotonous 9-5 job.

"That's what Jenna said, so I guess it must be true. Although she doesn't know anything about her grandfather because he left Isabella a long time ago. If she did, I would have something else to write about Isabella. But I am still happy with what I've found so far and I am looking for more leads."

"Well, you can always check the old Parish registers," Henry suggests.

"What's that?"

"Before the introduction of civil registration in 1855, Church of Scotland parish ministers and session clerks kept registers of proclamations of marriages. You might find something there."

"Wow, you're right. I don't know why I didn't think of that. I think I might need to go back to Luss again."

"No problem, you want to go today?"

"Yeah, I guess."

"You look a little upset, everything okay?"

I take a deep breath. "My mom dropped by unexpectedly and she can be a little annoying sometimes."

"Yeah, this is one of the reasons why I never go back home." He chuckles.

"She was so annoying. I didn't even have my breakfast this morning because of her, I am starving." I know Henry is my boss and I shouldn't be venting to him, but I just need someone to talk to right now.

"I haven't had breakfast either, you should come with me. I have a discount coupon for the African wrap place." It's hard to say no to a discount, so I agree. Before leaving, I feel Esme's eyes on me, but she doesn't say anything.

It's actually nice to eat with Henry. I get to tell him all about my problems and he patiently listens. "I am just worried about my cat. Mom doesn't like Olive at all," I tell him while chomping on my aubergine-hummus wrap.

"I didn't know you were a cat person," Henry says.

"I didn't know that either, but Olive is so cute, I can't help falling in love with her."

We keep lunch short since we both have to go back to work. After lunch, Henry goes back to the office and I find myself back on the train to Luss. Even though Luss is about an hour away from Glasgow, I don't mind the journey. The only problem is the trains get delayed sometimes and I am left waiting at the train station. Today is one such day. I am agonisingly waiting for any announcement about my train when an old lady comes and sits next to me. I am minding my own business when she starts screaming. Her screams take me aback. Other passengers stop and someone asks if she's okay but she's too busy screaming her lungs out.

"Is she with you?" someone asks but I tell them no. Emergency services are called and they're here in a jiffy. They put her on a stretcher and are taking her away when the woman stops screaming and looks at me.

"Lass, you don't have enough time," she says. I look around to see who she's talking to but then I realise she's talking to me. I don't have enough time? What's she talking about?

"She seems like a lunatic, the poor thing," I hear someone say and I nod. Just a lunatic mumbling things, I should pay it no mind.

I am still shaken by the incident when it's announced that my train is already at the platform. The Scottish countryside is full of large grass fields and sheep, it's very pleasing to look at. The beautiful scenery makes me forget about the incident that just happened. I find myself a single seat on the train. I'd rather not be around noisy people right now. I put on my earphones and put on some pleasant music. It's been such an eventful day and it isn't even noon yet.

As the train is waiting on the platform ready to go, I look out the window and notice a dark figure staring at me in the distance. It's hard to tell what or who it is, but my best guess is it's a woman. I feel my heartbeat increasing. It looks like she is the same woman I saw in the park the other day. She disappears in the crowd and when the crowd dissipates, she is not there anymore. It can't be. How can it be? This is the second time that I thought I saw Isabella. Was that Isabella?

I shake my head. I take my phone out and call Jenna. It might be Jenna, she looks exactly like her grandmother. Maybe she's following me around to see what I am doing. "Jenna, are you in Glasgow today?" I ask her as soon as she picks up the phone.

"No, I am not. Why? Do you need to ask me anything?"

"No, I thought I saw you," I say, unsure if she's telling the truth or not. She could be lying. But why would she lie?

"It must have been someone else since I am not there," she says.

"Okay. Apologies for disturbing you." I hang up the phone. I must have misunderstood it. It couldn't have been Isabella. It's just not possible.

Once the train reaches Luss, I head straight to the Local Family History Centres. It's a tattered old building where I don't think anyone ever goes. The insides of the building look old-fashioned, as if they've looked that way for ages. A jovial-looking woman is at the reception and when I go to her, she greets me. "You alright, hen?" she asks. She is old but warm, someone who'd be willing to help me.

"I am looking for some information. Would you be able to help me?"

"I'll do my best. What is it that you need?"

I explain everything to her and hand her the permission receipt that Henry signed for me. She inspects the permission slip and asks me to head to the top floor where all the records are.

"My colleague should be able to help you with what you need. What an interesting project that you're working on," she says with glee. If only she knew.

"Interesting it is. But..."

"But what?" I don't want to vent to this woman and make her think I am a lunatic. She seems like she's having a good day and I don't want to ruin it.

"Nothing. By the way, do you believe in witches?"

"Oh, I don't know. I am of the opinion that all kinds of things are possible in this world, both good and bad things."

I smile at her and leave her behind. I wish she'd said something along the lines of "Of course witches don't exist. What are you even on about?" or "These are just old stories that you shouldn't believe in." But she made me believe in possibilities. Possibilities of things that my logical mind says can't happen.

I climb the stairs and every stair creaks under my feet. It really is an old building that needs refurbishment. The top floor looks just like the top floor of any old library. It's full of books. So many histories are stored here and I get to read the big book of Isabella today. I almost feel like I am intruding on Isabella's privacy but I guess everything is fair in love and war and research.

I reach out to the woman working at the top floor and tell her about my project and research and show her my permission slip. She inspects the permission slip and asks me to follow her. She goes to a computer and types Isabella's name in a search bar. Once she has figured out the location of the rack, she takes me to an old book rack kept in the corner of the room and helps me find the records from the time Isabella could have been married. There are more than a hundred files.

"These are all the records we have from the time period you are looking for. I'll leave you to find whatever it is you're looking for," she says and gets back to her work. I look at all the old dusty record books in front of me and sigh. It will take me quite a while to get through them. By the time I've found what I came here to find, it's almost evening. My back is aching from sitting on the floor hunched up with books and my stomach is rumbling with hunger.

Covered in dust while sitting on the floor, my jaw almost drops when I spot Isabella Gowdie's name in the register. The font is tiny so it's difficult for me to read. I find a lamp on a table and keep the book under it. According to this, she was married to a man named Richard Gowdie. That's all the information the register has. Hours of research just to find her husband's name. It's not a lot but it's something. Usually, they don't write histories of women so it's difficult to find their old records but this Richard, I can find more about him. I go back to the lady who helped me find these records. "Thanks for pointing me in the right direction. I found the name of the husband and I was wondering if there are any records where I can find more information about him? His name is Richard Gowdie."

The lady takes off her glasses and ponders for a while. She then asks me to use the computer kept in the corner to locate the files myself this time instead of helping me find the right rack. I guess she is tired of me. But this is good for me too because now I can find whatever I want to find. Besides, searching on a computer would be much easier than going through each file in a rack.

While the building is old, I can tell the computer is new and it looks like it hasn't been used by many people. I type Richard Gowdie's name in the search box and wait for the results to pop up. I find a few files mentioning his name and the number of the rack where they are kept. I find his birth certificate but not his death certificate. It's still much easier than finding his marriage certificate. Isabella's death certificate is missing too. Could it be possible that Richard's dead body was also never found?

Whatever it is, I have done enough research for the day. I have been up since early morning and it has been a long day. I can't do any more work without my head exploding. I thank the lady and leave.

Where do I go from here now? Yes, I have Isabella's husband's name but how do I find out what happened between them? Jenna told me her grandfather abandoned his family? Did he know Isabella was a witch or did he leave them for some other reason? I doubt any record would have information about that.

I go back to the train station, ready to go back home. But something stops me. I just told myself that it's been a long day and it's time to call it a day. But I am not satisfied yet. I am curious to know Isabella's story. The more I find out about her, the more intrigued I am about what happened to her.

Instead of taking the train back to Glasgow, I take the train to Luss instead. I want to go back to her hut. There should be something there, something that I've overlooked so far. The sun is about to set when I reach there. It will be dark soon but I am not scared of going inside today even though I should be. I am curious and I won't be able to rest until I've quenched my curiosity.

Just like the last time, it's dusty and a musty smell surrounds the room. I sit on her bed and hang my head in my hands. I am exhausted. It's way past 5 p.m. and yet I can't stop myself from working, knowing fully well that I won't get paid for this extra time I am putting in. I didn't know my job was going to be this difficult. Perhaps my job as a waitress was indeed better. Although one of the reasons why I came here instead of going back home is because I want to avoid my mother for a few more minutes. I know she'll start bickering with me over small matters as soon as I step foot inside my flat.

I take a look around the hut, really look around. It's cosy and I wonder why it's been abandoned. It can easily become Jenna's holiday home or she can even put it on Airbnb for some extra cash. In fact, if she advertises the fact that the hut might be haunted, she can get extra money for it. Tourists love such shenanigans.

I have half a mind to just spend the night here. There is a comfortable bed and it isn't too cold in the hut. I look around the hut once again. There are cobwebs in the corner, and the walls are covered with mould but if I look at the floor, it isn't that dirty. This is strange.

I get up and inspect the floor, it looks as if someone has cleaned it recently. I bend down and see if there's someone under the bed again. Nothing. I check behind the mirror too, nothing there either. I get a strange feeling that there is something more to this hut than just a bed and a mirror. There is a small sink in the corner and a small space which is apparently a bathroom. I think I was wrong about the Airbnb suggestion. It is not a very pleasant place to stay at, it looks like a place someone would be forced to live in when they get shunned by society. I feel sympathy for Isabella. She had to live here alone without a family.

So far, I haven't found any records of crimes that might have been committed by her. Only rumours that she murdered people but that may not be true at all. The only reason people call her a witch is because she loved another woman. Sometimes I feel really glad I wasn't born in the past.

I lie down on the bed again, I am tired and in a desperate need of a nap since I woke up way too early today. If mom doesn't go away soon, I might just come and live here in Isabella's hut. I don't realise when I fall asleep but when I wake up and check the time, an hour has passed. There's no point in going back to the office anymore, I should just head back to my house. I do not look forward to seeing my mom again. I moved all the way up to a different country and somehow she still found a way to come after me. Shouldn't she be pestering Greg, her boyfriend all the time?

I take a deep breath and get up when I notice something strange lying on the floor. I look down to take a look at it. It's a piece of paper. I read it:

...feel happy again. Richard doesn't like me at all even though he said he loves me. He doesn't even look at me, just spends all his time in his study. Although I don't think I can complain. I don't like Richard either. I feel suffocated in this house with him. Perhaps I will ask the others for help, the coven always helps me.

I turn around the piece of paper to see if there's more but there isn't. The paper is exactly like one of the pages from Isabella's diary I found the other day. The paper wasn't there when I was awake. I would have seen it if it was.

Someone has been here, someone has been here when I was asleep. I feel goosebumps all over my arm, I need to get away from this hut. I take my bag and I run outside, turning around to have one last look at it. There is a picture of an eye on the door, an eye that wasn't there before. I take my phone out to take a photo and run away before anyone can see me.

People were right. Isabella's hut is actually haunted.

Chapter 5

I run back to the train station so disoriented that a kind lady sitting next to me in the waiting area has to ask if I am okay. I tell her I am fine but am I? I think it is clear that I no longer doubt whether Isabella was really a witch or not. I saw her twice today and then suddenly someone came to her hut while I was asleep. It wasn't Jenna, I made sure of that. It must have been Isabella. She's real and she's following me. I am no longer going to doubt myself and see things the way they are. I set her free the first time I went to her hut and since then, she's been after me. But what does she want?

So, I guess Jenna was right, there's no way out of this.

I suddenly have a splitting headache and I know going back home would only make it worse, thanks to my mother. I need to talk to someone, I need to get a drink. I take my phone out and call Hans.

"Hey, Kali," he says chirpily.

"Hey, Hans. I know this might be a little impromptu but I was wondering if you'd like to go for drinks tonight?"

"Uh... yeah, sure. Why not? But suddenly? What happened? Is everything okay?"

"Yeah, I guess. I am just looking for a bit of company tonight. Have had a long day. Although I'd understand if you aren't free."

"No, no. That's not what I meant. I should be done with work in an hour so I can meet you afterwards."

"Sounds good to me."

"Okay, I am currently in the city centre. If you are too, can we meet at 8 at Hillhead Book Club? Does that work for you?"

"Yeah, great. See you."

The prospect of meeting Hans makes me feel slightly better although I know Olive would be mad at me tonight. I will buy a special treat for her when I head home. I look up online to see what kind of place Hillhead Book Club is. From the pictures, it looks great. Even though Hans won't show up for at least another hour, I head there because I have nowhere else to go.

I order myself a burger and chips with a huge glass of beer. It's been a long day of research and I completely forgot to eat lunch today. I didn't even have a proper breakfast in the morning because I didn't finish my bowl of cereal in order to avoid my mother.

Food feels good after a long day. I am still shaken to know that someone, maybe Isabella, came inside the hut while I was asleep. Once I am done eating, I take out my phone to look at the picture of the eye I took earlier in the evening. I zoom in to closely look at the door but there's no mark on it, no sign of an eye. The door is unblemished. What is even happening to me anymore? Did I hallucinate the whole thing? My hands begin to shake. I am not sure what's real and what isn't real anymore.

I have to order two more beers just to clear my mind and calm my nerves down. While I needed to learn about Isabella for my job, it is becoming clearer to me now that I need to learn more about her to understand what's happening to me. It's no longer just work, it's personal now.

But where do I go from here? I think of the woman I met the first time I went to Isabella's hut. She could tell me something, she is a local and knows stories. Yes, I should go back to see her next week. I can ask her about Richard Gowdie this time and maybe even Jenna. She was the first person who tried to warn me about this whole mess but I didn't listen to her. Maybe she can still help me.

I am munching on my chips while mulling over everything when Hans appears.

"Hey." I wave at him. He is wearing a black blazer over a white shirt and black trousers. A formal attire, he must be coming straight from work.

"Hey, Kali. Looks like you began without me," he says while pointing to my two empty beer glasses.

"Oh, I just came an hour earlier and I was really hungry. I hope you don't mind."

"Why would I mind? Although I hope you would still have a few more beers with me. This week has been... rough. I am really happy that you called me and asked me out for drinks."

"Yeah, I wasn't sure if you'd be able to come."

"Of course, I'd come. Do you know that you are the first girl ever who has asked me to get drinks first? I was impressed."

"Just like you, I have had quite a day and I needed a beer. Hence this." I point to my two empty glasses.

"Let's drink some more."

Hans summons the waitress and some more beer is on our way for us. "So, tell me about your day," I ask.

"Apologies for my language but my boss is an arsehole. When he is mad, he makes our lives hell. That's what happened. And to make matters worse, my favourite football team lost today. Do you watch football?"

"No," I shake my head. "Sorry." Every guy I've ever dated has been into football, a game I can't bring myself to care about at all.

"It's alright. I guess I should stop watching too, I spend too much time being worried and stressed out rather than actually enjoying the game." The waitress serves us the beer. We clink our glasses and drink up. "So, what's going on with you?" Hans asks.

"Where do I begin, Hans?" I definitely can't tell him about seeing a witch so telling him about my day is a little bit difficult. I just focus on my mother which is where my day went to shit. "Well, my mom arrived unexpectedly last night and let's just say I don't have the most cordial relationship with her." I am trying to be as vague as possible because there's no other way to talk about my mother. How do I tell a new person in my life about the person who's been a nuisance to me for twenty-two years of my life?

"Oh, yikes. Would it be rude of me to ask why?"

I look up, realising that even I don't know the answer to that question. "I actually don't know, Hans. I have heard mothers love their children and take care of them. That's not my mother. It has never been like that."

"I am sorry."

"Your mother seems quite nice." I want to change the topic. Talking about my mother is too depressing, especially when I have downed a few drinks.

"Yeah, I have to admit my mom is pretty cool. She is a single mother and she worked hard her whole life to make sure I could go to a university. She is a superhero, Kali. Really."

I shift in my seat. Is it wrong to feel jealous? I wish I had a mother like Betty. A mother who cares about her child. "How did your father die?" The alcohol in me is making me braver to ask questions that I wouldn't have asked otherwise.

"He passed away in a car accident. He was a good man, I still miss him. What's with your father? Is he in the picture?"

The smile on my face vanishes. "No, Hans. I have got the worst of both worlds. My parents divorced while I was young. They told me they just stopped loving each other but I am pretty sure they never loved each other in the first place. I was sixteen when that happened. My dad still calls me occasionally on birthdays and festivals but whenever he does, it's awkward."

"When was the last time you met him?"

"It's been years. He travels a lot, I think he is in the Philippines currently."

"Both our lives are quite sad, I think I need another beer. What about you?"

I know that I am starting to get quite drunk. On a scale of 1 to 10, I think I am at 7. "What the hell, it's a Friday night. We should just drink until we are puking our guts out."

"I agree."

And that's what we do. As the night gets darker, I lose track of how much beer I have in me. Thankfully, Hans is much more composed than I am.

"You are completely smashed, aren't you?" he asks.

"Oh, yes. Oh yes, I am." Even the waitress is judging me by how much I have drunk which is why I leave her a big tip when we get the bill.

"Should we go?" Hans asks.

"I don't want to but I have to."

"What do you mean?"

"My mom will be there and it's almost midnight. She is going to judge me so much for being out so late."

"Well, you are an adult. You don't have to tell her every time you go out."

"That's not what she thinks, Hans. She thinks she still owns me. For my whole life, she has made me feel guilty because she fed me and paid for my other expenses. You don't understand what living with her feels like." If you don't have a mother like that, it's difficult for anyone to understand how I feel when it comes to my mother. My eyes get teary and I am no longer as happy as I was a few moments ago.

"Kali, are you alright?" I feel guilty for breaking down in front of Hans. I try to compose myself. It's embarrassing.

"I am alright, I just need to go to the toilet."

He nods. I leave him and rush to the toilet to cry some more. I am like one of those girls who drink too much and then cry about their ex-boyfriends but instead of boys, I am crying about my mommy. I feel pathetic. When I get up from the toilet seat, I feel dizzy. I have drunk way too much, more than I realised. It feels like I am not even in my own body.

I splash some water on my face hoping it would help me. When I open my eyes, I see a woman standing behind me. I should scream,

I should run, I should call for help. Instead, I feel relieved. Because it tells me that what my mind thought was true is actually true. I am not going crazy. I wasn't imagining things. I was right.

It's Isabella.

"Isabella?"

She is wearing a black dress and her hair and makeup is perfect. It doesn't look like she has been dead for several years now. She looks the same way she does in the photograph I saw of her. She looks the same age too even though she clearly can't be in early 20s. "Good evening, Kali."

"You're not real, are you?" I mumble. There's no one else in the toilet, I am alone here. I hope someone walks into the toilet and tells me that I am talking to the air, that there's no one in this toilet apart from me. But I am alone and I know that the woman standing before me is real. As real as I am.

"You already know the answer." She's smiling at me, as if it's just a casual girl's day and we are out for coffee. It doesn't seem like she's here to harm me. If she wanted to hurt me, she would have already done so. There's something that makes me like her, even pity her. She looks innocent, she doesn't look like a scary ghost who's running after me to murder me.

"What's going on, Isabella? What the hell is going on?" And I genuinely want to know the answer. I have so many questions in my mind and I don't even know where to begin or if it's even the right time to ask questions. Hans is waiting for me outside. How would I explain to him what I am seeing right now? How would I explain this to anyone? I am struggling to understand this myself.

"Kali, you don't have to suffer. You can leave everything behind. Come join me, come join us."

"Suffer? I am not suffering. I am quite happy in my life." And I realise that I am not lying. I am genuinely really happy with my life.

"You know what I mean. You can leave all of this behind and come join us." She offers her hand to me as if she's calling me to hold my hand. I am not sure if I want to do that.

"What are you talking about? I am not going to join whatever it is that you're asking me to join. I am not even sure what you're asking of me, Isabella." My throat is parched even though I've had plenty of drinks throughout the evening.

She giggles like a little girl. "Oh, Kali. You are too innocent."

The way she's looking at me, the way she's smiling at me, I feel uncomfortable. I am not scared but I don't want to be in this room with her either. I want to leave, I want to escape.

"I am leaving," I tell her.

"Kali, please think about it. You can leave all of this behind and come join us." Once again she repeats her words without telling me specifically what she's talking about. She is just repeating herself without telling me what it is she is inviting me to join. What does she think? I'll leave my whole life behind and do whatever it is a strange woman in a public toilet asks me to do? She should have been smarter than this.

Having a discussion with her is going to be futile which is why I decide to disregard her and leave behind. I open the door and slam it shut. When I look behind, the door stays shut and she doesn't follow me. Outside the toilet's door, the pub is just the way it was a few minutes ago. People are sitting around tables with their friends, laughing, joking and drinking. A waitress walks across me looking at me strangely but then she gets back to her work. Another woman goes inside the toilet but I assume Isabella isn't there anymore. Or maybe she is. I don't want to go back inside to find out.

Hans is still sitting at the table, checking his phone. I walk to him and he looks up.

"I am ready to go," I tell him and I am truly ready to go. I don't want to be in this pub any second longer.

"Are you okay? You look a bit... different." He holds my hands.

"Different? What do you mean? I am perfectly fine." Now this is a lie but I don't know what else to tell Hans.

"You look a bit shaken. And I thought I heard a scream inside the toilet. What was that about?"

"Scream? I heard no scream."

"Are you sure? I am sure the whole pub heard it. Everyone was looking at the door and a waitress even went to check inside."

"What? No one came inside."

Hans looks a bit confused. "Alright. It doesn't matter. You sure you're okay? You really do look a bit shaken."

"I am fine, Hans. Just a bit exhausted as I told you before. Let's call an Uber, I am ready to go home."

I take my phone out but he asks me to put it back once he sees that I am struggling to even unlock it. I must have drunk too much. He takes his own phone out and calls a taxi.

It's raining outside. Not raining so much that it'd get you drenched but raining enough to make you feel cold. I shiver and feel Hans's arm wrapping around my body. "Wow, so romantic," I tell Hans. I don't know why I am pretending that everything is fine right now. I just saw a woman who should be dead right now in the toilet. But I guess I don't want to think about it right now. I am too drunk and tired right now.

"Just making sure you aren't cold," he says.

The taxi is quick to arrive. I rest my head against Hans's shoulder and wait for this day to be over already. Too much has happened today. I feel Hans's hand rubbing my arm. The ride home is probably only around twenty minutes but it feels like it's been ages.

Once the taxi drops us off, I am relieved. "Okay, good night." I am not in the mood for elaborate goodbyes.

"Kali, are you sure you're okay?" Hans asks once again and with the way he's looking at me, I can tell that he's genuinely concerned.

"I am already at my house, Hans. I just need my bed and I should be fine."

"I know but just with your mother, I hope you won't fight too much with her. You are not in the right headspace right now." I almost forgot that I'd have to face another witch as soon as I get home. I am really not in the mood to talk to my mother right now, who I am sure would be curious why I was out so late in the night. Nonetheless, I don't want to burden Hans with my problems.

"Hans, don't worry about me. I will never be in the right headspace to deal with her. But I promise I'll be fine tonight and if I am not feeling okay, I'll call you. Does that sound good?"

Hans nods. "Yes, good night, Kali. Thanks for a lovely night. I hope we'll do this again soon."

I turn around and walk to my building all the while feeling his stare on my back. I put my keys in and come back to a dark house. I tiptoe while I open my door, the lights are switched off and I don't turn them on again just in case I wake my mother. I put my jacket behind the door and take off my shoes as silently as I can. If I wake her up, it'll be another argument that I am not in the mood for right now.

I have to turn on the torch on my phone and I go inside my bedroom. It's strange that my mother slept without even calling me and asking me where I am. She usually doesn't do that. Whenever I was out late at night during uni, she always called me to ask about my whereabouts. It used to be very annoying and she never stopped doing it no matter how many times I told her not to do it. This is why I am really surprised that she didn't do it today. Maybe this is one habit that she has changed.

Olive gets up when she sees me and wraps herself around my leg.

"Hey, Olive. I am sorry I stayed out so late," I whisper to her and scratch her ears. I take her in my arms and go to the kitchen to see if she's had her dinner or not and I am relieved to see her bowl empty.

I peek inside my mother's bedroom because I can't believe she slept without pestering me. I open the door slightly and even though it's dark, I can tell there's no one in the bedroom. I turn on the light and I am right, my mother is not there. She is not in the living room either. That means she just hasn't come back yet from wherever she went. I was fretting for no reason at all.

But where did she even go? She said she was going to spend the day with her friends. Now it's me who's slightly worried about my mother's whereabouts. I take my phone out and send her a message. "Where are you?" I wait for a few moments hoping she responds but she doesn't. She was never a big texter so I am not surprised.

I go and lie down on my bed again while Olive lies next to me. Where is my mother? Should I be worried? Perhaps not. When I was a child, she would often leave me alone in the house without any food for many hours. She is an adult woman, she must be fine. I turn off my lights and go to sleep. I am exhausted and don't want to worry about one more thing.

I wake up the next day feeling exactly how one feels after a night of heavy drinking. I drink some water and check the time. It's 10 a.m. I don't feel as good as I'd like to feel when I wake up but I still feel way better than I did last night. It really was a long day and the night of drinking helped to take the edge off a little bit. I think about Hans and a smile spreads on my face. I am so glad that I met him. I don't know what lies ahead of us but I am enjoying whatever is going right now between us.

I wake up famished and pour myself some cereal and milk. I finish it in a few minutes and then peek into my mother's bedroom. She still isn't home. Olive is lying on her bed and I know that if my mom knew that Olive was there, she'd start another argument with me. But I don't disturb Olive. I put her food in the bowl and take it to her. While she eats, I take out my phone and call my mother.

She picks up after a few rings. "Mom, where are you?"

"Good morning, Kali. I am with a friend right now, she asked me to stay with her last night since it had already got too late and the neighbourhood you live in is full of criminals." Her voice is extra sweet which probably means whoever she is with is around while she's talking to me. She never speaks to me this politely unless someone is around us or she's trying to ask me for something. But who is it? I am really curious now. My mom never went over for sleepovers with anyone but now this sudden change?

"Which friend is this?" I ask.

"Oh, sweety. You don't know her but she's wonderful. We are planning to go shopping together and then on a whisky tour," she responds in that extra sweet tone once again that makes me want to puke.

"You don't even like whisky, Mom."

"I am in Scotland, Kali! I want to experience everything this country has to offer. Now, stop pestering me." She hangs up the phone. I have no idea what's going on with my mother. I am very curious about her new life and her friends but at the same time, I am glad she's not home. I get a day for myself without her nagging.

I go back to my room and decide to spend some time with Olive since I left her alone last night for far too long. I am scratching her back when memories from last night come back to me. The piece of paper that was left in the hut. The pub's toilet and Isabella appearing and asking me to join her. Just the memory of her raises my goosebumps.

There is a part of me that wants to believe that last night didn't happen at all. I was drunk and wasn't thinking clearly. I could have hallucinated and imagined the whole thing. Hans said someone screamed. Maybe I imagined everything.

But no. I know that I wasn't just being drunk. Even when I am drunk, I am very capable of being in my senses. No, it's not possible that I imagined the whole thing. I was drunk but I was still in my senses. I saw her and spoke to her. She was real.

Isabella asked me to join her and I couldn't understand what she was asking of me. But I think I now know what she wants. She wants me to join her coven. That's what Jenna and Courtney had told me. I am quite curious about the whole thing. What would being a part of the coven mean? What do witches exactly do? Are witches harmless? If I join the coven, would I also get to live like Isabella for many years? I have never been a part of a club or a group like this so it might be nice to be a part of something, I'd get to make friends. But I don't know if joining Isabella's coven would be the right thing. Even thinking about it makes me feel uneasy.

I am giving Olive a massage while thinking about all of this when I hear a knock on my door. I open it to find Hans smiling at me.

"Hey, Kali." I let him in. I am still in my pyjamas and my hair is very messy. I didn't even wash my face before going to bed last night so yesterday's makeup should still be there on my face, although smudged. I am feeling very conscious about the way I look right now but I am still very happy to see Hans.

"Hey, Hans."

"Sorry for dropping by without texting you but to be honest, I was a little worried about you after last night."

"Oh, Hans. I am fine, really. I was just exhausted last night but now I'm feeling a lot better."

"That's good. Anyway, there's another reason why I came here so early in the morning. Our Uber driver from last night called me, he said he found this in the car and thought it belonged to us. It isn't mine, is it yours?" There's a necklace in his hand, a necklace with a pendant in the shape of an eye. The same eye I saw on Isabella's door. I take it from him. "Is it yours?" Hans asks me again.

"Yes, it's mine. It must have fallen off last night." I have never seen this necklace before but I know that somehow this necklace belongs to me.

"I am glad you've got it back now. It looks very pretty."

"Yeah, I was wearing it last night and it must have fallen off last night in the car. Anyway, let's talk about you. I feel like I keep blabbering about myself and my problems all the time. You must get bored. How are you feeling this morning?"

"Hey, I like hearing about you. You can talk to me about your problems all day long and I still wouldn't get bored. But yeah, I am okay. Slightly hungover but not too bad."

"Oh, yeah. You drank too much last night," I say. He is looking around the house as if searching for something. He must be looking for my mother.

"My mom's not around," I tell him. "She wasn't even home last night when I got home, I was worried for no reason at all."

"Oh, really? Where did she go?"

"That's the thing. I have no idea where she went or who she's with. All I know is that she's fine, I just spoke to her on the phone a while ago."

"Well, that's good."

"I am sorry, Hans. You just wanted to relax last night and I got way too drunk."

"It's okay, it's okay. We've all had those nights. In fact, seeing you so drunk was a little bit funny. You're funny when you're so drunk."

"I am funny when I am sober too, you'll see."

"Really? You should take me out again and this time there will be no alcohol. Just you and me. Make me laugh," he says.

"Sure, I have to. How about right now?"

"Right now? You really like to be spontaneous, don't you?"

"I just don't like waiting."

"Well, if you're ready, I am ready."

"I am actually not ready. I still have to take a shower but I won't be long."

"Okay, I am willing to wait." I open a packet of biscuits and leave it with him in the living room along with Olive. Olive is surprisingly really friendly with him and deposits herself in his lap.

I rush to my bathroom. I know nothing might happen today but if it does, I want to be prepared. So I shave my legs and even between my legs. Just in case. I also wear my best dress, the one that looks good on me and some light makeup. I look at the necklace Hans just gave me. It's clearly not mine but it's pretty and matches with my dress so I wear it. I spontaneously asked Hans to go out with me but I don't know what we'd do today. Whatever it is, I'd really like a day just to relax for a bit and today seems like a perfect day to do that.

"You look really nice," Hans says when he sees me.

"Thanks." My blood rushes to my cheeks. I can't even remember the last time someone complimented me on my looks.

"So, where are you taking me?" he asks. It's difficult to think about because I don't know a lot of places in Glasgow, I am still new. One thing I do know is that wherever I am going has to be cat-friendly. I am not leaving Olive alone today, I have left her alone for long hours for the past couple of days. I want to pamper her today.

"Do you want to go to the botanical gardens?" I ask. I have never been to botanical gardens myself but it's one of the places that come up on Google at the top when you search Glasgow so it must be good. Besides, it's difficult to get bored while spending a day in any of the gardens.

"Yeah, sure. It's one of my favourite places in the city. Although if you plan to take Olive, it may not be the perfect place," he says.

I feel a little deflated knowing that. I thought I had come up with something. "Oh, then where should we go?"

Hans thinks for a moment. "Let's drive out of the city. We can go to Loch Lomond, it's really beautiful there and since it's sunny outside, Olive would enjoy it too. We can buy some food from Tesco and have a little picnic."

"Sounds better than my plan."

I put Olive in her carrier along with some of her toys. We both go to Hans's house to get his car and then drive away. I see the city leaving behind and soon we're outside where everything around us is green. The view is beautiful and I am thankful for the peace. The city's hustle and bustle was getting too much for me. There is a comfortable silence in the car where neither of us feel awkward with it.

"Want me to play some music?" Hans asks, breaking my reverie of thoughts.

"Hans, did you say that you heard me yelling in the toilet last night?"

"Well, I don't know if it was you or if it was a yell. It was a really loud sound, like a woman screaming. It could have been you but I am not sure. Why? Why are you still thinking about that?"

"I… I don't know. I just find it a bit strange that you thought you heard someone screaming."

"Could have come from somewhere else? You were alone in the toilet, right?"

"Yes. Yes, I was alone," I lie to him because I don't want to believe in the truth myself.

"Yeah, you got me really worried for a second. But when you came out, you were fine. I just assumed you must have seen a cockroach or something."

"I won't scream if I see a cockroach, I can assure you that."

"It's okay, don't worry too much. You were really drunk, as I said."

"I am sorry."

"Oh, pssh. Stop apologising. Last night was a fun night for me. You kept joking you were seeing spirits, I think you even called yourself a witch at some point."

"What? What are you talking about? None of this happened. I would have remembered it if it had happened."

"Oh come on. Stop playing around."

"I am not!" I say seriously but Hans thinks I am joking. I look outside the window, I don't remember any of what he is talking about. I have been drunk before but I know that I don't forget everything I do when I drink so much.

I feel Hans's other hand holding my hand. "Don't worry so much about yesterday. Think about today, we're going to have so much fun." I look at him and smile. I don't want to ruin Hans's day and more than that, I don't want to ruin my own day by overthinking about all of this. It's a day-off for me and I just want to relax for a bit. I can't stress myself while being surrounded by so much beauty.

We reach our destination after driving for an hour. We park the car, get our bags out and find a nice spot by the loch. It's a sunny day and there are several people who have come here to enjoy the day. Olive falls asleep as soon as we sit and I let her. If this is what brings her happiness then so be it.

Hans pours prosecco in two glasses and hands one to me. I take a sip and feel my stress leaving my body. Being surrounded by water on a sunny day with my cat and a friend. This is the perfect way to spend a day when you're not working.

"Were you dating anyone while you were in Birmingham, Kali?" Hans asks me out of the blue.

"Yeah, I was seeing a couple of people casually but was never serious about any of them. Just never really found 'the one', you know."

"People? Not men?" he asks with his eyebrows raised.

I shrug. "I don't think I have figured out my sexuality yet. I went on a few dates with women and honestly, those dates were better. I don't really have a label to identify myself but I am open to all kinds of experiences. But personally, I have had better experiences with women than men."

"Really? Why?" He turns around his whole body towards me. He is really interested in this conversation, I can tell.

"It's hard to explain. Women try harder, that's all. Or maybe the guys I went on dates with were douches."

"What about me? Do you think I am a douche?" he asks playfully. I look into his dark grey eyes.

"It's too soon for that to know, I guess. Time will tell."

"What do you think would happen to us though?"

"I think we have a shot but I don't want to rush into anything already. I like taking things slow." I know that rushing into relationships only leads to disaster. I like going with the flow. If things between me and Hans are supposed to work out, they will.

"By the way, do you know how tall I am?" Hans asks and takes a bite out of an apple.

"I don't know, you seem way taller than I am. 6'1?"

"I am 6'3." He winks.

"Oh god. I am only 5'3, one whole foot shorter than you."

"Oh wow. How do you feel about that?"

"You're a giant. It's good though. You can help me get stuff down from the top shelf," I say playfully and chuckle.

"Well, that's true. You can help me pick up stuff from the floor." We both laugh. "Anyway, what's your usual type of guy?"

"I'll tell you what my type used to be. Tall: 5'10 to 6'3. Intelligent. At least an undergraduate degree. Funny. Good banter, meme collection etc."

"Okay, not funny. You're just describing me now." He rolls his eyes playfully and looks very cute while doing that. I am charmed.

"But I am moving away from physical features. What's my type now is one who can communicate well, is trustworthy and mature."

"I like short 5'3 Indian girls, who like to learn about witches and have a pretty face." I playfully hit him on the arm.

"I know you like me."

"It's definitely good to move away from physical attraction but you've gotta have an initial spark, I reckon. Also I'm in your old height range so I'm acceptable."

"You're definitely more than acceptable. Besides, both ugly and handsome men have broken my heart. I may as well go for the hot guys."

"I couldn't agree more. So if I am more than acceptable, am I allowed to kiss you?" he asks while raising one eyebrow. It's a question I have been waiting for him to ask me for a while.

"Yes, you are allowed." He leans into me and plants a kiss on my lips. Olive wakes up and starts scratching Hans's stomach.

He laughs. "Someone's jealous."

"Oh, Olive." I lift her up and kiss her on her cheeks. Why is she so cute?

Hans and I spend the afternoon just chatting about random things. I feel very comfortable to be just myself while I am around him. I don't feel like I have to pretend to be some other cooler version of myself, I can just be me. The way he looks at me while talking to me, I can tell that he likes me too.

When we've had enough of the sun, we decide to get up and find a quaint cat-friendly cafe where we head to for a snack. We order paninis and some coffee and at the end, Hans gets a small slice of chocolate cake. "This is for celebrating that we are dating and our first kiss," he says. We both share it. The cafe also has some food for Olive and by the end of it, she seems satisfied.

"We must come here again, Olive really likes this place, I think."

He nods. "We'll definitely come here again. It's quite a memorable place for us now."

We head back outside to enjoy the last rays of the sun as it begins setting down. We find a bench to see the setting sun and Hans wraps me in his arms again and it feels cosy. Olive climbs and sits between us so that she is cosy too.

"You are so clingy, Olive." She merely blinks at me in response. I don't realise when the day has passed by. It was a good day and I didn't have any thoughts about work either. By the end of the day, I feel refreshed, although still reluctant to go home.

As we drive back to the city, all I am thinking about is how I don't want this day to end. It's too nice, it's my best day in Glasgow so far.

"You're still up for the Isle of Skye trip, right?" Hans asks me as we are nearing Govan. To be honest, I had completely forgotten about the trip and that I was even invited. Nonetheless, I am always ready to go on a holiday.

"Of course, I am still up for it. When are you guys going?"

"Next weekend. We leave on Friday evening and will be back by Sunday evening. We'll drive there. Two of my friends are joining us. They're both super nice so don't worry about hanging out with new people."

"Don't worry about me. I love meeting new people." And that's true. I have a dearth of friends right now and it'd be nice to make new friendships.

"That's good, then. I am so looking forward to you meeting my friends. You'd like them. They're really close to me so it's important you approve of them."

"Would they like me back?" I ask.

"Why not? You're amazing. Who wouldn't like you?" I chuckle.

The drive home is seemingly shorter than the morning's drive. Perhaps because I am not looking forward to going back home. Hans drops me and Olive outside my flat. He bends down to kiss me again as he's saying goodbye.

By the time I am inside my flat, there's a huge smile on my face. A smile that I find difficult to wipe off. I am hanging my coat on the door when I hear my mother calling out my name.

"Yeah?" I shout back.

"You're back?"

"Well, clearly," I say while shrugging.

Her interrogation begins. "Who was that?" she asks while rushing to the kitchen window and seeing Hans's car driving away. She seems very, very curious but I refuse to quench her curiosity.

"What are you talking about?" I pretend I don't understand her question. This is how I survived my teenage years, by pretending I have no idea what's happening around me. This is how I am going to survive while my mother's here too.

"That man whose car you just got out of," she says as if it's obvious.

"He is Hans."

"Hans who? I've never heard of him before." She crosses her arms.

I leave her standing behind and go into my room. I say, "He's a new friend. I have loads of friends now who you don't know about."

She follows me behind. "This boy? Are you dating him?"

"Yeah." I shrug.

"Is he a good boy? Does he have money?" That's what the most important thing to my mother is when it comes to relationships. It's always been money. She was an immigrant in this country and didn't have much money when she came here. This is why she married my father, because he had more money than her. That, and also his stronger passport. She never loved him but only pretended that she did in the beginning. Perhaps she wants me to follow the same path as her. I'd rather stay single and alone forever than do what she did.

Besides, I have a well-paying job myself so I don't need to marry someone I can't tolerate simply for money.

"I don't know." And I really don't know how much money he has. I know that he works as a lawyer and by the state of his flat, I can tell that he lives a comfortable life. We've never discussed our finances in detail because it is too early for that.

"You don't know? Then you should find out before wasting your time with him."

I lie down on my bed and stare at the ceiling. I'd rather not have this conversation right now. "Mom, please. Don't tell me who I should date or not. It's not like you've had many successful relationships yourself."

"Kali!" That's all she says because she doesn't have any other answer. She can't tell me I am wrong or I've said something that's not true. We both know I am right.

"Leave all of that. Let's talk about you. Where have you been since yesterday?" I sit upright.

My mother looks away as she responds. "I was with my friend, how many times have I told you?"

"What friend? I didn't know you have friends in this city. You never told me about them before."

"Why do you want to know? You've never been curious about my life before." This time, it's she who's right. I've never been curious about her life because I never had to. She always told me about everything going on in her life whether I wanted to hear or not. But now she is starting to keep secrets. But I am not going to give up so easily. I want to know who and where she's been hanging out with.

"Well, I am making an effort now. So, tell me. Where have you been?"

She walks to the living room and I follow her. This time it's she who's trying to avoid me. "I went to the beach." A beach? As far I know, there's no beach in Glasgow. She must have gone outside the city. But why? It's not even warm right now. Why she'd go to the beach when the days are getting shorter and chillier. It makes no sense and it isn't something like my mother usually does. So, it must have been her friends who took her there.

"Who did you go with?"

"A friend. She's very nice."

"Really? Which friend? Did one of your friends from Birmingham move here? Is it Selena, the woman who lived next door to us? I think she is half-Scottish."

"No, it's not her. I haven't spoken to that woman in ages. I made a new friend when I came to this city. I met her at the train station before you came." A new friend? My mother met a woman at the train station and decided to spend two days and one night with her? I can't believe this. But I can tell that my mother is telling the truth.

"Did you just spend a whole night with a stranger who you met at the train station?" I can't believe my mother can be so naive.

"Oh, Kali. Why are you after me? I can take care of myself. I know how to choose my friends, I am not like you."

"You're not like me? What's that supposed to mean?"

"You know what I am talking about? You've never had any sense who to choose as your friend."

I stand there dumbfounded, not knowing what to say. I know what she's talking about now. She is talking about the time when my best friend got pregnant when we were teenagers. She never stopped complaining about how I should stop talking to her and no longer be her friend simply because she had been careless.

I leave my mother and shut my door. I do not want to speak to her. If she gets murdered by a stranger she met at the train station, she gets murdered. I do not care. I shut my eyes trying to calm myself down when I hear the sound of my door opening once again.

"Kali, tell me about your boyfriend."

Oh, so it's her turn again for interrogation. I get up and look at her. She does not want to tell me about her friend but she wants to know everything about my guy. Perhaps it was a mistake letting her know that I am dating someone but I know that telling her I am single would also not stop her from talking my ear off. "His name is Hans and he is a lawyer." I want to keep it brief. I don't want to let her know anything about him, I don't want to tell her how I feel for him. It's personal information and I don't think she's close enough to me to know such things about me.

"A lawyer? Interesting." She pauses for a moment. Perhaps she's trying to search in her memories if she knows any lawyer or any information about how much money they make. "Although you must be wary of him. If you end up getting married and then file for divorce, you won't get even a penny from him. Lawyers are very cunning." I can't believe my mother is thinking of my divorce even before I have got married. I don't even know if I'll get married to him.

"Don't worry, Mum. My marriage will be better than yours." I wasn't trying to hurt her but the way her jaw hangs open, I know that I have.

"How could you have said such a thing to your mother? You know what I've been through, what your father put me through." She's starting to get angry now. I have really crossed the line with that statement, I can tell.

"I am sorry, I shouldn't have said that." I really am sorry. Even though she is snarky and mean to me, I don't want to stoop down to her level. I know she's had a difficult life and I don't want to rub that in her face.

"Kali, I don't know why you continue to hurt me when I have sacrificed my whole life just for the sake of your happiness. No matter how much I do for you, you never appreciate me. You always try to prove I am the villain in every situation. I was a single mother, doing my best to raise you. And every day, you remind me that even giving birth to you was a mistake."

If I had known that she would rant so much, I would have just shut up. I apologise once again but she just shuts the door and leaves. I hear her muttering something through the thin wall of my room. I can hear that she's saying that she should never have had a daughter and that she should have given me up for adoption. I also hear my father mentioned somewhere in the rant.

I shut my eyes and lie down. It's something I've heard many times in my life before so it shouldn't sting me as much as it does. I have always known that my father never really wanted a child but my mother convinced him. And then they had me while already being in a very tumultuous relationship hoping it would fix everything. But it didn't. So, I continued to exist as a failure. I couldn't keep my parents together. I couldn't fix everything that was wrong in their relationship. When my parents divorced, there was no reason for me to continue existing. But I had. My mother never got to really live her life because of me. And somehow whatever is wrong in her life is my fault.

Half an hour passes before the house is silent again. My mother is not muttering anymore and my tears have dried up too. I think about how just a few hours ago I was so happy. I thought with Hans in my life, things might start to finally get better now. But I don't think anything would get better as long as I continue to have my mother in my life.

***

Sunday passed by and my mother didn't talk to me at all. I didn't try to talk to her either. We've had these phases before. When I was 14, my mother didn't talk to me for one whole year except when she really had to. It was very awkward but over the years, I have got used to such phases. I should really enjoy these phases but for some reason, I can't. I am feeling guilty right now. But at the same time, I think things are better this way. My mother and I should not talk to each other. Our relationship is so damaged, it can't be saved anymore. It could never have been saved and I am slowly coming to terms with that. I spend Sunday going for a walk and then getting lunch by myself at one of the restaurants nearby. My day was punctuated by Hans's text messages, which is perhaps the only thing going right in my life right now.

Thankfully Monday arrives and I get to go outside again. I don't have to be around my mother and my work will distract me. Through this whole mess, I didn't even get time to think about Isabella and everything that happened on Friday night. Every cloud has a silver lining, I guess.

When I see Henry and Esme in the office, I feel so relieved. Familiar faces who don't hate me are always something I appreciate. I go to my computer, ready to dive into my work.

"Hey, we are going to write up what we are going to speak at the conference and then practise all of that. Is that okay?" Henry asks.

"Sure."

I go to my computer to pull up my word document with all my notes but I can't find them on my drive anymore. How can this be? I go to the Recycle Bin and they aren't there either. I tell Henry about it.

"It's strange, are you sure you didn't accidentally delete the file?"

"Yes, I am sure." I would have remembered that if I did something like that. I may not be a technologically whiz kid but I know how to not delete a file, at least. My first thought goes to Isabella but then I shake my head. I can't keep blaming her for all the problems in my life.

"Does that mean you have lost your research?" Henry asks, three wrinkles appearing on his forehead. Henry may be nice but I know that he takes his work very seriously. Losing your research work like this would be a gargantuan mistake, which is why I have made many, many copies of all my work, both digital as well as physical.

"No, I took a printout of all my findings last week so I still have them on paper. I always back up my research."

Henry's forehead wrinkles disappear. "That's good. The computer must have glitched or something." I nod. That should be it. Henry goes back to his desk but I am left wondering where my document file went. If I hadn't taken a printout, I would have lost months' worth of research.

"We're going to practise our parts after lunch," Henry tells me.

I spend the day preparing my speech. Even though it's just three minutes, it is still stressful since I have to make sure I say everything about Isabella I have found so far in just three minutes. I want to make sure I am objective while describing her. I am trying to tell her story but I am not sure if she's the protagonist of her story or the antagonist. So far, I haven't found anything about her that makes her look bad. Even when she met me in the pub's toilet, she didn't hurt me or say anything rude to me. I have no reason to believe that she is an evil witch as of now. But I am 100% sure that she is a witch.

After lunch, we all gather around in a circle and practise our speeches a few times. The work all of us have done so far is commendable. I hear about the witches everyone else is researching about but I am sure that no one is more interesting than Isabella. Everyone talks about women who were falsely accused of being witches. They were innocent women. But they were not witches. Or if they were, there's no way to prove that. Except when it comes to Isabella, she's a real witch. Whether she's innocent or not, I am yet to find out.

Henry claps when we are done with practising. "I am really proud of you girls. The History Department will have no other option than to give us more funding for this project. We can continue studying about witches for the next year, maybe even after that. That is really great."

I am glad Henry is happy. I am not sure if I'd like to continue working here for a long time. I enjoy this job but I am getting invested too much in my work. I work more than my assigned hours and I am getting haunted by my work. I'd rather not have a witch appear in my life. Besides, there aren't enough resources on Isabella apart from rumours and superstitions. I can't get on the stage during the conference and tell people that I saw Isabella while I was drunk in a pub. The History Department will shut down this project if I say that. Maybe they'll send me to a hospital after hearing that.

I am back on my computer reading a research essay on modern-day witchcraft when I get an email from Courtney. I have to think for a moment who Courtney is when I remember she is the blogger who I contacted to find out more about Isabella. I had almost forgotten about her.

Hey Kali,

I hope your research is going well. I just wanted to invite you to our monthly meeting tonight. A few of us witches who are interested in witchcraft gather together and learn some spells. Since you're researching all of this, I thought it'd be interesting for you. Let me know if you'd like to come. Here's the address.

Courtney

I type the address in Google maps and see that the meeting is happening just ten minutes from our office at night. I tell Henry and as expected, he is enthusiastic about it. Not just Henry, Esme, Natacha and Lisa are excited as well. "You should go, it'll be so cool," Lisa says.

"Are you sure? These women call themselves witches but I am sure they just pull tarot cards in front of a candle."

"Even if they do just that, it can be an important part of this research. Esme found out about some rituals the other day and if you go to this meeting tonight, you'll find out about how these rituals are performed today. We can compare and contrast the two time periods." While what Henry is saying is true, I don't want to work overtime tonight but I do not have a polite way of saying that. "If you go to this meeting, you can take an extra holiday any day this month and of course you'll be paid for the extra hours you put in."

That's all I wanted to hear. As long as I am financially compensated for my work, I am happy to do it. "Alright, Henry. I'll go. How bad can it be?"

"What time is it?" he asks.

I check Courtney's mail again. It's at 11 p.m. Why meet at such a late hour? Does magic not work during the day? It's something I'll definitely ask them tonight. I quickly shoot Courtney a quick email that I'd be there. Since I have to go meet them at 11, Henry lets me go back home earlier.

At home, I prepare for my meeting tonight. Maybe attending this meeting of witches might help me learn something about Isabella. I am not sure what I should wear tonight but I'd like to look like a witch too. But I am not really sure what witches look like. I think of Isabella and what she was wearing when I saw her. She was wearing a black dress. I am going to copy her look as closely as I can.

I look through my clothes and find a black dress that I once bought for a Halloween costume. I even used to have a witch's hat but I didn't bring it to Glasgow from Birmingham. I never thought I'd need it but life surprises you sometimes.

"You are back from your office already?" My mother asks when I go to the kitchen to get something to eat. She wasn't talking to me until morning but now she's back to being her old self. I thought her non-talking phase would last a little longer.

"Yeah, I have to go for a meeting tonight so they let me go early," I tell her without looking at her.

"Meeting tonight? What kind of place do you work at that they send you to work at night? I thought you were working for a university."

"It doesn't usually happen. An interesting event is happening tonight and I have to go there to make connections." I don't tell her that I am going to meet witches, she'd probably have a heart attack if I tell her that.

"Kali, you never told me. What kind of job do you have?" It strikes me that it is indeed true that I never told my mother about my job. She has no idea what I do for a living.

"I am a research assistant at the University of Glasgow. I work for the History Department."

She nods slowly chewing my words, I am pretty sure she is still clueless about what I do. "So, does that mean you are researching some historical event?"

"Yeah," I look away, focusing on some crisps that I am eating before leaving. I don't want to answer any more of her questions.

"What are you researching?" She sits next to me on my bed.

I do my best to hide my frustration and clear my throat. "I am researching Scottish women."

"What's so special about these women?" She's understandably confused. She probably can tell that I don't want to discuss this with her which is why she's prodding me even more.

"These women were accused of being witches," I say nonchalantly but I already brace myself for her outburst.

"Witches? Kali, are you serious?" She can't believe what she just heard.

"Why? What's wrong?" I ask.

"I don't want you to spend all your day studying black magic. Witches can be dangerous. Well, some of them."

"Mum, you do realise that witches don't exist right? I mean, not the kind of witches that you see in movies and TV shows," I say without conviction. If I told her about Isabella, she'd go insane.

"Witches do exist, my friend told me about them. Although she did say that some witches are nice, I hope you are researching them and not the evil ones who sell their souls to Satan."

"No one sells their souls to Satan. That's just stupid. Besides, how does your friend seem to know so much about witches?"

"She knows about everything. Even though she is much younger than I am, she understands me."

"How much younger?" I still have no idea about the people my mother is hanging out with. I thought she's hanging out with women her own age, perhaps a knitting club or a hikers group. But no, it's something else.

"She is about the same age as you. But being with her makes me feel what having a good daughter really feels like," she says.

I leave my bag of crisps on the table and get up. Of course, she'd always find a way to put me down. I go to the bathroom to wash my hands when I see the necklace Hans found in the Uber. I put it around my neck, it is so creepy it matches with all of my dresses. I feel something brushing against my leg, it's Olive. She is looking at me as if she is accusing me of something.

"Do you want to come with me?" I ask and she only purrs. I guess the other girls won't mind if I bring Olive, popular culture shows that witches like cats, especially the black ones. I put her in her carrier and take her along with me.

"Are you taking that dirty cat with you?" my mother asks as she sees me leaving.

"Her name is Olive and yes, I am taking her with me. I don't think she likes being around you." I shut the door behind me before my mother can find something repulsive to say.

I still don't know if I can take Olive in the subway so I call an Uber. I don't know why I agreed to meet Courtney, she is a woman I have never met before. I hope she isn't too crazy although I doubt she wouldn't be. I am a little nervous about the whole thing. It's a group of strangers and I am going to their house. What if something goes wrong?

I buzz Courtney's door when I reach and she lets me in. The first thing that I notice about Courtney is her hair. It's bright red. I have never seen her before, except for the tiny picture she has set for her thumbnail, which is how I recognise her bright red hair. "Courtney?" I ask and she nods. She is wearing a similar dress to mine; although, with her tattoo-covered arms and neck, she looks much cooler than I do.

"Kali! You came!" She seems surprised as if she didn't actually believe that I'd show up. I have half a mind to turn back but I don't. I am being paid for these hours and I'll have to tell Henry about everything that is going to happen tonight. I just can't leave.

Before entering, I point to Olive's carrier. "I brought my cat with me, I hope you don't mind."

"Oh, no problem. Although I must warn you that I have a dog. Don't worry, I'll lock him in the other room so your cat would be comfortable. What's her name?"

"Olive."

"Like the colour?"

"Like the fruit." She laughs and takes me upstairs.

Courtney's house looks normal, I expected her to have Halloween-like decorations but it's quite similar to mine. I don't know why I have such prejudices about women who call themselves witches. Perhaps I am too judgemental. These are women like me.

She introduces me to other women in the room. There are quite a few of them so I forget their names as soon as they introduce themselves. "Kali is doing research on witches so I thought it'd be great for us to get some popularity." She giggles and so do the other girls. Is this why Courtney invited me today? So that she can be popular? It does make sense now. She probably just wants her blog to have more readers. Something tells me tonight is going to be a very long night.

"Do you have any questions for us?" one of the girls asks.

"Oh, no. Just continue doing whatever you usually do. I'm going to sit in the corner silently with my cat and you can pretend that I am invisible. I'll just be here making my notes and I'll ask you a question if anything comes to my mind."

"Would you like something, Kali? Perhaps a drink?" Courtney asks and I shake my head to say no. The last time I got drunk, Isabella appeared before me. Who knows what might happen tonight?

I put myself in a chair in the corner and take Olive out from her carrier. Olive looks around the room to examine where she is. Some of the girls squeal at the sight of Olive and beckon her to them. Olive is very friendly with them. The girls love my cat and want to play with her but Courtney asks them not to.

"Girls, we can play with Olive once we have done our ritual. It'll be midnight soon. We shouldn't be wasting any more time." I bring Olive back to me. We shouldn't be disturbing these girls while they are doing their ritual. Olive sits next to me in the chair and she seems just as confused as I am. I have no idea what this ritual is going to be. I take out my MacBook and wait for them to continue.

The girls sit around in a circle while holding each other's hands. There's a candle and some tarot cards in the middle of the circle. I roll my eyes, of course, they have tarot cards. I have read several essays in the last few days and I am pretty sure no witch ever used tarot cards and candles for their hexes and spells. But as soon as this thought pops up in my head, I reprimand myself. I am not going to be judgemental and let these innocent women do whatever they want to do. They aren't hurting anybody and if doing this brings them happiness, why should I judge them for it?

Courtney hands everyone a pen and paper. "Girls, tonight we are going to practise how to make our wishes come true. I learnt this trick from my mother. We have to write whatever we want on a piece of paper and then bury it in the garden outside in the moonlight. Whatever we write will come true by the next full moon. It's called the law of attraction." The girls enthusiastically get to write. I have heard of this law of attraction before but I am highly doubtful it's this easy to make your wishes come true. Or is it?

Courtney looks at me. "Kali, do you have any wish that you'd like to come true?"

"I— I, uh, I am okay, Courtney. Thanks anyway."

"Oh, come on, Kali. There's no harm in just writing down your wish, come join us. Trust me, you aren't selling your soul to anybody just by writing down your wish." She laughs and I chuckle too nervously. I never said that but I am sure these women are used to such jokes being made about them.

I suppose she is right after all, what's the harm in writing down what I want? I join their circle and Courtney hands me a pen and a piece of paper. There are several wishes that I'd like to come true. I'd like to be a millionaire, no—a billionaire and I'd like to go on a world tour and I'd love to date a Hollywood actor. Perhaps Henry Cavill. But clearly, none of these things has the possibility of coming true in the next twenty-eight days.

I have heard of the law of attraction before, it's not something that only witches use. I have always questioned the possibility of it being true or not but I guess I can test it today. So, I have to be practical while I am trying to manifest something. I think for a moment and then I write down: *I want my salary to increase.* This is something I'd really appreciate. Money is the only thing I want in my life right now. Everything else falls into place as soon as someone gets rich.

I fold the paper and then Courtney takes us all out in the garden under the full moon. "Now just bury the paper in the soil," Courtney says. I dig some soil with my hands and make a little hole. I put the piece of paper in the hole as if I am planting a seed. I cover the hole back with the soil. My hands are covered in the dirt and so is everyone else's. We go back upstairs and wash our hands.

I am thinking of leaving now that the ritual is completed but Courtney doesn't let me. "We are only beginning!" Just the beginning? What else are they going to do tonight?

I am glad I decided to stay because Courtney brings out seven glasses of red wine. I didn't know witches loved alcohol so much. I told myself earlier that I wouldn't drink tonight but I can't resist. One glass wouldn't hurt.

"This wine tastes so different, what is it?" I ask Courtney after taking a sip.

"It's a secret, just enjoy." She winks at me. I put the glass away because I am sure I am not going to drink something mysterious among a group of strangers. To make sure Courtney doesn't get offended, I sneak into her bathroom and spill all of it. The red liquid leaves stains all over her basin that I wash off with water. Whatever this is, it's not wine.

"Courtney, take out your Ouija board," one of the girls suggests and the other girls cheer.

"Alright, alright." Courtney disappears in her bedroom and comes out with a big box. They again sit in a circle and when I don't, they look at me.

"I am okay, here. I don't want to be a part of this," I tell them. Writing a wish on a paper is one thing but an Ouija board? There's no chance I am going near that thing. I was expecting Olive to sit next to me and but to my surprise, Olive sits inside their circle sniffing the box.

"Your cat is much braver than you are," a girl with glasses says to me.

I fake a laugh but I am not amused. Brave? They think I am scared. And I hate to admit this but they are right. I am scared. So far I have determined that these things don't work but what if this Ouija board changes my beliefs?

Courtney turns the light off and lights some more candles. She places them around the room. "So, who do we want to call today?" she asks as she sits in the circle again.

"Let's call Beira," someone suggests.

"Beira who?" someone else asks.

"You don't know Beira? She is one of the strongest goddesses of Scotland."

"No, we don't want to call a goddess, we should call a witch who can guide us."

I don't know why I am writing all of this in my notes, none of this is helpful. These girls are just drunk and they seem to think they are witches. I doubt Isabella ever drank wine and played with an Ouija board.

"We should call my grandma Ruth, she was a part of a witch's coven." Courtney looks up to me. "She was a part of Isabella's coven."

"Oh, wow," I say because I assume Courtney is expecting some kind of reaction from me. And I would indeed be amazed if grandma Ruth can tell me anything about Isabella.

The girls together put their hands on the triangular pointer while Courtney says, "Grandmother Ruth, we summon you. Guide us on the path of becoming great witches like you were. Let us know you are here."

I move a little closer to see if the triangle is moving or not. The triangle moves to yes. The girls gasp but I highly doubt that spirit moved this triangle, it must be the girls themselves.

"Did any of you move the triangle?" I ask.

"No," they all say in unison. I do not trust their response.

Courtney speaks, "Grandma Ruth, Kali here doesn't believe that you are actually here. So, I am going to ask you a question that might help her. Were you a part of Isabella's coven?"

The triangle moves to yes and Courtney looks up at me with a smirk on her face.

"Was Isabella evil?" I ask, not believing that I am actually talking to a piece of wood.

The triangle moves to yes again. I get up and go closer to their circle.

"Grandma Ruth, is Isabella still alive?" I ask.

The triangle moves to yes again. I am getting tired of this, clearly these drunk girls are moving the pointer by themselves.

"Grandma Ruth, did Isabella love her husband?" I know the answer to the question which is why I ask this. The triangle moves to yes and this is how I know this ritual is bogus and I no longer want to be in the same room with the girls. Isabella hated her husband and it was something she shared with her coven. "Grandmother Ruth" should have known this.

"Alright, I think I should leave. You girls go ahead," I say abruptly, surprising everyone in the room.

"What? Why?" Courtney asks.

"This is just a board game, Courtney. Your grandma Ruth isn't actually speaking to us. She didn't know the answer to the last question. It was wrong. Isabella didn't love her husband."

The triangle moves to 'goodbye' and the girls look at me as if I drove Ruth away. Courtney switches on the light. "You can leave if you want to, Kali. I am not going to force you. Even if you don't believe in any of this, at least you could have an open mind and not hurt our feelings by discrediting our beliefs." Courtney's words make me feel guilty. I do agree that I am being a spoilsport tonight.

"I am sorry, I was rude. I shouldn't have said that."

"It's alright. I guess witchcraft is not your cup of tea, some girls are just ordinary. There's nothing wrong with that." I am not sure if Courtney is trying to insult me or not but I ignore her comment.

I take out my phone to look for a taxi around but there are no available taxis on the app. I tell Courtney and she says, "Yeah, it can be difficult to find one at this time. Keep waiting."

I nod. While I am waiting, one by one the other girls leave after bidding me and Olive goodbye. I can tell none of them is happy that I don't believe in their rituals. When all of them leave, Courtney comes and sits next to me.

"I am sorry if I ruined your night," I tell her. I really am sorry. I should have come here with an open mind. But I already decided that these women aren't witches even before coming here.

"Don't worry, you didn't. Have you found a taxi yet?" Courtney smiles at me.

"No, no cars here." I am starting to get worried now, I don't think I can walk back home in the middle of the night. And the subway should be closed too.

"Look, keep searching if you want but finding taxis in this area is not usually easy. I should have thought of this before inviting you. I have an extra bed in my bedroom, you can sleep on it. I have no problem if you want to stay over tonight. I know I am a stranger but you can trust me." I don't like sleeping in other people's houses, especially someone I met a few hours ago but it's starting to seem that I don't have another option. I continue staring at my phone screen hoping a taxi would appear but it doesn't.

"Alright, I am so sorry I am such a nuisance to you," I tell Courtney.

"Oh, you aren't. I am glad you are staying, to be honest. I can tell you more about us witches through the night. I won't lie, I invited you here so that my blog could get more publicity. But I don't want you to write rubbish about us. I would love to enlighten you more about the modern witches and our ways."

"Sounds like a plan. Thanks for letting me stay. It's the least I can do for you after offending you and your coven."

"Come in, I will give you something more comfortable to wear. Oh, by the way, what are you going to do with Olive?"

"Huh? What do you mean? She's just going to sleep in the same bed as me. That's what she usually does anyway."

"Yeah, well. I told you my dog is in my bedroom."

"Oh." I look at Olive. "I think she can sleep alone in the living room."

"Cool, come inside." She takes me inside her bedroom. I turn around to look at Olive and I can tell she is not pleased that I am betraying her for a bed. "Sorry, Olive," I mouth at her but she turns her back to me clearly expressing that she is angry.

Courtney's dog is a German Shepherd who starts barking at me as soon as I am in the room.

"Don't be scared, he just wants to sniff you." I let him sniff me while standing in complete fear. He is a giant dog compared to my little Olive. He sniffs me and then goes back to sitting on Courtney's bed.

Courtney gives me a long, orange T-shirt and matching shorts. It's not the kind of clothes I usually wear but considering the circumstances, I accept them. I turn my back around and change into these clothes. When I turn around, Courtney is also changing into her pyjamas.

"What do you think?" I show Courtney my new clothes.

"They fit you so well."

"They do."

"What's that around your neck?"

I look down to see what she's talking about. My necklace is lying on top of my T-shirt. "It's my necklace," I tell her.

"I can see that it's a necklace but where did you get it?" she asks.

"Why? Why do you ask? I got it from a charity shop in Govan," I lie to her.

She comes closer to me and inspects it. "I have seen this symbol before, this eye. I can't remember it now. Do you know what it means?"

I shrug. "I think it's just an eye. I wore it because it matches my dress."

"It's almost 2 a.m. We should go to bed," Courtney says while still looking at my necklace.

I nod and lie down on the bed. Courtney leaves a small lamp turned on while she sleeps. "I am scared of sleeping in the dark," she says. A witch who is scared of sleeping in the dark. Interesting.

I close my eyes but the light from the lamp is disturbing me and I have become used to sleeping with my cat now. Not having her in the same bed as me makes me feel like I am incomplete. I close my eyes hoping to drift into sleep but I feel something wet on my hand. It's Courtney's dog licking my hand. I pat him on his head hoping this would make him go away but he doesn't. He climbs on my bed and wraps himself around my legs. Just a few minutes before he was barking at me and now he wants to sleep on top of me? Sharing my single bed with him is even more uncomfortable. He is way too big and I am very uncomfortable lying under him.

I toss and turn around but eventually give up. I don't think I'd be sleeping tonight. I have always struggled with sleeping in new places and this cramped bed with a big dog doesn't help. I get up to see if Olive is sleeping well outside and find her on top of the Ouija box sniffing at it. "You're still awake, Olive?" I guess even she doesn't like sleeping in a stranger's house. I take her into my arms and see that the triangle on the Ouija board is missing. I look around and find it lying on the floor. I put it back and I am about to put the Ouija board back in its box when the triangle moves.

I look around the room to see if there's anyone else besides me, if there's anything that's strange but nothing. There's absolutely nothing that's touching the triangle and it is somehow moving on its own. It moves to D, then O, N, T, B, E, S, C, A, R, E, D.

Olive growls at the board. "Don't be scared," I say out loud. I can't believe what's happening in front of me, should I be scared? I should be. I should be scared and go back to bed and forget that this ever happened. But instead, I stay and ask a question.

"Are witches real?"

The triangle moves to 'yes.' This time there's no one even touching the triangle. I gulp. Grandma Ruth is here, I guess.

"Is Courtney a real witch?" "No." I knew it, Courtney can't really practise magic. Even her Grandma Ruth thinks that.

"Grandma Ruth." I clear my throat. "Were you in Isabella's coven? What was it like?"

I wait for the triangle to move. I, A, M, N, O, T, R, U, T, H. It isn't Ruth.

I look at Olive in confusion. "Then who are you?" I, S, A, B, E, L, L, A.

I take a deep breath. "Isabella, why are you following me? What do you want from me?" I, W, A, N, T, T, O, T, H, A, N, K, Y, O, U.

"Thank me? You don't have to. I freed you by mistake, it wasn't something I purposely did. You can leave me alone, you don't have to continue to haunt me." N, O.

Before I can say something else, the triangle points to "goodbye". "Isabella? Isabella? Come back." But the triangle doesn't budge. Isabella is gone. I put the board back in its box and lie down on the sofa with Olive on top of me. I stay awake the rest of the night.

***

I must have drifted into sleep at some point because I wake up with Courtney shaking my arm. "Kali, are you asleep?" I bolt upright and rub my eyes. "I was but now I am awake."

"Oh, I am sorry. I didn't want to wake you but I have to take Zeus downstairs for his morning walk and we have to pass through here."

"Zeus?"

"My dog. And why did you sleep outside? Was there a problem with the bed inside?"

"No, Courtney. I just wanted to be with Olive."

"Oh okay. I'll bring Zeus outside and you can wait with Olive there." She points to a door, which I assume is her bathroom.

"Sure," I take Olive in my arms and hide in the bathroom as Courtney passes through the living room. When I hear the door click, I come out. I check the time, it's not even 6 a.m. yet. Not having slept the whole night, I do not feel like going to work today at all. But then I remember that if I don't go to work, I would have to stay at home with my mother and I'd rather stab my eyes than do that. Once Courtney returns, I change back into my dress and give her clothes back.

"Thanks for lending them to me."

"I remember now. I remember where I've seen this necklace before," she says after she has locked Zeus in the room inside.

"Do you?"

She goes to her bedside table and takes out a picture from the drawer. "Yes, yes. I knew it."

"What are you talking about, Courtney?"

She hands me the picture. "Here, see it for yourself."

It's a black-and-white picture of her family. I see her old little self in someone's arms who I presume is her mother. I scan the photo with my eyes when I see what she is talking about. An old lady is wearing the same necklace that I am wearing right now. It's the same symbol that she's wearing.

"Is that your grandmother?" I ask.

"Yes. That's my Grandma Ruth."

***

"How was last night?" Henry asks as he sees me sitting at my desk. I left Courtney in the morning, rushed to my flat to shower and get dressed. I still came two hours late but Henry excused that since I told him I had to spend the entire night with Courtney last night. In fact, he applauded that I am willing to put in so many extra hours for work. He also assured me that I was going to get paid for all the extra hours too.

"Last night was... it was interesting." That's all I can say to describe last night's events. There are so many things that I am still processing and I can only tell Henry everything once I know what exactly is happening.

"Interesting?" Henry repeats.

"Well, they did play with tarot cards and candles but they also played with an Ouija board. I found out that Courtney's grandmother was also a part of Isabella's coven. So, I guess I have another lead to follow this week." I keep my explanation brief enough that it would satisfy Henry.

"That's great. I have to say, you are working the hardest out of all the girls and you have made the most progress," Henry says while beaming.

"Have I?" I ask doubtfully but deep down, I know that it might be true.

"Yes, I want to reward you for this amazing work," Henry says.

"You don't have to, Henry. I am just doing my job."

"I know, I know. But let me, please?"

I nod. "Alright, what are you planning?"

"Would you like to go for lunch with me?" Lunch with Henry? I want to say no. I don't want to go with him but I don't know what excuse to make right now. When he sees me pondering, he says, "Come on, Kali. It's just a professional lunch. Let me treat you." A professional lunch? That makes me feel slightly better. There's nothing wrong with having a professional lunch with your supervisor.

"Okay, sure. When do you want to go?"

"How about today? I know of a nice place nearby."

"Okay, I'll see you at lunch."

I get back to making notes about last night on my computer as Henry gets back to his own computer. I turn around and catch Natacha winking at me. Why is she doing this? I ignore her and focus on my work at hand. Lunch is still two hours away and I have lots of work to do before then.

Courtney told me her grandmother's full name was Ruth Maeston. It's Ruth Maeston that I need to look up now since I couldn't find anything about Isabella's husband. I hope I will find something about Ruth in the archives. According to Courtney, she was a witch too. I am sure there must be something about her that is worth adding to my research.

Henry comes to me earlier than usual for lunch. "Isn't it a bit early?" I ask but he waves his hand.

"No one's looking, just come."

I shut off my computer and leave with Henry while feeling guilty that I get to leave early while my colleagues don't. I should talk to them more often lest they start to hate me.

"Where are we going?" I ask Henry once we are out.

"There's a Mexican restaurant nearby, do you like Mexican food?"

"I love it." And right now, I can eat whatever is in front of me. I haven't been much interested in food for the past few days. All my focus has been on my work, Olive, Hans and my mother. I am badly in need of some time just for myself.

The restaurant is only a few minutes away and unsurprisingly, is quite busy at this time of the day. We find a table in the corner and order some quesadillas and tacos.

"Would you like a beer?" Henry asks.

"It's the middle of the day," I tell him.

"It's Scotland, we don't have to wait until night for drinks."

"Nah, I am not in the mood. I didn't sleep last night at all and I have a headache. I think I'll just drink diet coke."

Henry orders a beer for himself. After placing the order, he crosses his arms, leans into his chair and then looks at me with a smile on his face. "So, tell me what's going on with you. It seems almost ages since we all went out for drinks last time. Tell me everything."

"You're right. It does feel like ages ago."

"We all should do something like that again, we should do something this weekend to celebrate."

"Well, I am going away from Glasgow this weekend but perhaps when I am back, sure. Maybe next weekend."

"Oh, you're not free this weekend. Where are you going?"

The waiter brings our food punctuating our conversation. "The Isle of Skye," I say after taking a sip of diet coke.

"Oh, wow. That's a beautiful place. Who are you going with?" Henry asks.

"I am going with a guy that I am dating and his friends. I have never been there before so I am really excited. We are driving there."

Henry stops chewing his taco and looks at me. "You're dating someone?"

"Yeah," I say while blushing. Hans sent me a kiss emoji this morning and I know that might not be a really big thing, it felt good. He is the only normal thing in my life right now.

"Who are you dating?" Henry puts his taco down and looks at me with his brows furrowed. I don't like the way he is looking at me. I also don't think I want to discuss my private life with him. We're colleagues after all, not friends. But I don't know how to evade this question so I answer truthfully.

"Just a guy who lives two doors down from me. His name is Hans."

"You know, I was hoping to ask you out." This time it's me who puts her food down.

"Henry, you and I can't be dating. We work together, that'd be so inappropriate and it would make our colleagues uncomfortable."

"I don't think it would. Are you serious about this Hans guy?"

"I... I don't know why we are talking about my dating life, Henry." I am very, very uncomfortable with the way Henry is behaving right now.

"Oh, come on. Tell me. Are you serious about him?" Henry asks impatiently. It seems the only way to shut him up and leave me alone is by actually answering his question.

"We've only been dating for a few days, I don't know where this will go," I tell him and regret it instantly. I should have told him that I am very much serious about Hans.

My answer seems to make him feel better. "That's good, then. I think it's just a fling you'd be over soon. And are you exclusively dating each other?"

"I... I don't know about him but I am not seeing anybody else."

A smile appears on his face. "Once you break up with him, would you like to go out with me?" I can't believe Henry just asked me this. Suddenly I am no longer in the mood to eat anymore. This is highly unprofessional and I didn't expect this from him.

"Henry, I can't promise you anything at this moment," I tell him. The truth is I wouldn't go out with him even if I wasn't dating someone else. I am not interested in him that way and besides, he is my supervisor. Us dating each other would make it very awkward for everyone else in the team.

"No problem," he says. I don't think he understands what I am trying to say.

He continues eating his taco as if we didn't talk about anything awkward. It's difficult for me to stomach my food down after this. I don't like Henry, not at all. Even if I were single, I would not date him. Especially after this conversation, I have no interest in him. I wait for him to finish his food so that we can leave.

"You're not eating anymore?" he asks when he sees that I am not even touching my food anymore.

I pick up my taco and finish it in three bites as a response. Henry chuckles at me. "When you're my girlfriend, you won't be allowed to eat like this. It's bad manners." Allowed to eat? What kind of creep is this guy? Thankfully, he finishes his food soon and asks for the bill. I take out my wallet to pay but he waves his hand. "It's my treat." I guess the least he can do after this horrible lunch is pay £10 for my food.

"Would you like to go eat some frozen yogurt?"

"No, Henry. I don't like yogurt. I think we should just head back to the office," I tell him. I don't want to be alone with him for even a second. I'd like to go back to my computer and pretend none of this happened.

He agrees and we head back. I spend the rest of the day staying away from him. I stay focused on my computer and pretend Henry doesn't exist. I know avoiding Henry isn't a solution and I'll have to do something about this situation. I'll need to talk to him and make my feelings clear that I am not interested. I think of quitting my job but no, I can't do that. I need this job. Besides, why should I quit my job? I didn't do anything inappropriate.

I'll need to think about this later. Right now, all my focus is on Isabella.

Chapter 6

I am extremely happy when the weekend comes and the Isle of Skye trip is finally here. Now I get to finally explore Scotland, which is embarrassingly something I haven't had the opportunity to do yet. I leave Saturday morning and won't be back until Sunday night. I am more than glad to be away from work since I won't have to face Henry. Besides, I'd heard so much about the Isle of Skye even before moving here. One of the reasons why I moved to this country was because of the scenic beauty and I hate that I haven't had the opportunity to explore it yet.

"Mom, will you take care of Olive while I am away?" I ask when I am about to leave. I know I should have made arrangements for Olive beforehand but I sometimes forget that I have a cat. Yes, I love having Olive around me but I need to be more responsible which is not something I like. Besides, I purposely left asking if Mom would take care of Olive for the last moment because I didn't want to let her know that I am going away. She's been here for a while and hasn't shown any sign that she's in the mood to leave soon. It's like she's moved in with me permanently. I hope she hasn't. I have no idea what she does most of the day. She doesn't have a job and lives on her savings. I don't know much about her boyfriend but I do know that he's extremely wealthy. Perhaps he sends her money every week.

I often wonder about Greg. What did he even see in my mother? My mother isn't pretty nor is she pleasant to be around. But I did hear that Greg is an immigrant from some third-world country. Perhaps he is with my mother to get that spouse visa. I genuinely can't understand why anyone would want to be with my mother willingly.

"Mom, will you take care of Olive?" I ask again as she didn't hear me the first time. She has her headphones on and is shaking her head pretty vigorously while lying on her bed.

"What?" she asks while taking her headphones off and staring at me as if I just interrupted her meditation session.

"This is the third time I'm asking you. I need to be away for a while. Will you take care of Olive while I am gone?"

"Where are you going?" she asks. She goes back to staring at her phone. She's smiling at her phone. I take a step forward to steal a peek at her phone. I can see that she's video-calling someone but can't make out who it is.

"I am going to the Isle of Skye for a two-day trip. Didn't I tell you about it?" I know that I didn't tell her about it but I am going to pretend that I did. "I am going with Hans and his friends. We are driving up there."

"No, you did not. Why are you going? When are you leaving?" She looks up.

"Tomorrow morning and I'll be back the day after in the evening. And what do you mean why? Why do people take vacations? Why did you come here from Birmingham? I've always wanted to travel around a bit and now that I have a job, I can finally afford to do it." This reminds me of the times in my childhood when my mother denied me even the simplest pleasures in life if it cost money. I was never allowed to buy expensive dresses or chocolates, even for special occasions. It wasn't even that my mother didn't have money. She did have money and she was spending all of that money on herself. I shake my head. I am not going to get lost in these sad, old memories. Now is not the time for that.

"That sounds nice, Kali. I'd like to come with you."

"Come with me? What are you talking about? I am going there with the guy I am dating and his friends. I can't take you with me." I scoff. I can't believe she thinks she can hang out with me and my friends. She should hang out with her own friends.

"Calm down, Kali. I just made a joke."

"It wasn't very funny. Anyway, you still haven't answered my question. Will you take care of Olive while I am gone? She's pretty easy to take care of and I can't take her with me."

"Take care of Olive? Me?" She can't believe I just asked her this question.

"Yes. Olive's food is on the bottom shelf of the kitchen cupboard. You just have to put it in her bowl, give her water and clean her litter box. She doesn't want much. She's a very nice cat."

"Clean her what? Honey, I am not going to do that. Your cat is disgusting. I have said it before and I'll say it again, you should put her in the bin. I am not going to take care of her."

"What? Why?" I should have known that she wouldn't do it for me. I don't even know why I expected that she would.

"Oh my lovely daughter, you should never have adopted a cat if you can't take care of her. Besides, I have plans of my own this weekend." Now I am intrigued.

"Where are you going?" I ask pretending I am not interested but I am.

"Not that I need to tell you everything but I am going to Edinburgh with my friend. You hang out with your friends and don't tell me anything about them. Then how can you ask anything about my life?" I sometimes think my mother is a teenager and she never grew up mentally.

"Alright, fine. I will find some other arrangements for Olive." Now, what am I going to do with her? I don't know. I don't think I should leave her alone in the house.

"You should just leave her at the bin you picked up from, black cats aren't really meant to be kept inside a house," she repeats what she's told me multiple times before. She's convinced that Olive is a symbol of evil and shouldn't be in this house. If there's anyone who needs to leave, it's her. Not my sweet Olive.

"Thanks for the suggestion," I say and shut the door in her face. I take a deep breath and look at Olive. "What am I going to do with you? Do you just want to come on the trip with me?" I am not sure Olive would enjoy that. She likes staying at home, curled up on my bed. I don't know if she'd like to be away from home for one whole weekend. I also don't want to miss this trip. Oh, I should have known that there are some cons to having a pet. This is one of them. I am also keeping a cat in the house even though the girl I am subletting from told me pets aren't allowed. If she finds out somehow, I might get into trouble. But that's something I don't need to worry about right now. I need to find alternate arrangements for Olive.

I call Hans. Maybe he'll have any idea of what I should do. I don't want to bother him too much with my life problems but I can't think of anything else right now.

"So what should I do? I can't leave her behind," I finish telling him about everything that just happened with my mother. "I don't know why but I thought my mother wouldn't have too much problem taking care of her. She not only said no but she also suggested I should put Olive in the bin."

Hans laughs. "Your mother is something. But don't worry. My mom can take care of Olive, she'd be really happy spending time with a cat," he says. "She was telling me the other day that she misses spending time with animals after retiring."

"Really?" I can't believe that I have found a solution to my problems within a minute.

"Oh, yeah. We'll just drop Olive and her stuff on the way tomorrow. My mum would love to spend a weekend with Olive."

"Thank you, Hans. You really saved me here." I breathe a sigh of relief.

"No problem. Finding solutions to your problems is my job now. Anyway, are you done with packing?"

I look at my clothes thrown all over the floor. "I am almost done," I tell him. It will be chillier up there so I need to pack some warm clothes. I am also making an attempt of fitting all my stuff in a small bag so I don't take up too much space in Hans's car.

"Awesome, I'll see you tomorrow."

I get to packing, first my own stuff and then Olive's. I am quite excited about this trip. Not only because I am going to a new place but because I'll get to hang out with some friendly people. I hate to say this but I have been missing hanging out with people my age for a while. I am young, I should be having fun! This trip will be fun, it will have to be. I have been looking forward to it for so long. I am not going to let anyone ruin it for me.

***

"Hey." Hans kisses my cheek and lets me in. I am at his house, ready to drop Olive at his mother's house and then drive away with him to pick up his friend.

"You ready?" he asks.

I nod. "Yes. I am so excited."

"Me too."

"You know, I am nervous about meeting your friends," I say as Hans carries my small suitcase to his car while I carry Olive's stuff and Olive herself.

"They are nice people, they'd like you. There's nothing to be nervous about. Was your mother happy that you're going away for the weekend?" he asks. By now, he understands my mother and her shenanigans very well.

"I think she just thinks I am spoiled and wasting my salary away on a trip like this. She's herself spending the weekend in Edinburgh. I have no idea how she made friends so quickly," I tell him.

"Is she going to stay with you for long?"

"I hope not. I have tried asking when she'd leave but she just always dodges the question by saying something mean."

"You won't have to face her for the next two days. Rejoice." He kisses me on the top of my nose. I put Olive's cage in the backseat and we leave.

Hans parks the car in Betty's driveway and then we walk to Betty's door. Hans knocks. A few minutes pass but the door doesn't open.

"Did you tell her that we are coming over?" I ask as he knocks on the door again. We both find this strange that Betty doesn't come to the door.

"Of course I did. She was so excited to spend the weekend with Olive, I think she even bought a new toy for her. This is strange."

Hans knocks on the door again. Silence.

"I think you should try calling her," I suggest. Where did Betty go?

He takes out his phone and calls her but she doesn't pick up. "Something is wrong," he says. Something does feel wrong indeed.

"Do you have an extra key?" I am starting to think that Betty might be in trouble.

"I do, it's in my car. You wait here." I see Hans walking towards the car and coming back with a set of keys in hand. He opens the door but it's dark inside.

"Mum?" He switches on the light and we find Betty lying on the floor. We both run to her to make sure she is okay. Betty is lying in her own vomit. There are even a few spots of blood near her head.

"Oh my god, what is wrong with her?" I ask but Hans is too shaken up to respond. He just shakes Betty to wake her up. Betty blinks and we both heave a sigh of relief.

"Mom, what's all this? Are you alright?" Hans asks frantically. Betty's hair is messed up and even though we know she's conscious now, she seems very weak. She looks around the house as if she's wondering where she is. She stares at him and then at me and then back at him. "Oh, Hans. I am alright." We both help her stand up and take her to bed.

I hand her a glass of water while Hans takes off her shoes and wraps her in the blanket. She drinks it and then looks at Hans. "I am hungry."

Hans gets up but I make him stop. "You should stay here with her, I will cook something."

He nods and says, "There's a packet of soup in the cupboard. Just add some hot water and bring it."

I go to the kitchen and I find the packet of soup. I add hot water to it, pour it into the bowl and take it to Betty. Hans takes it from me and feeds it to Betty himself. I take Olive out of her cage and hug her tightly while she tries to wriggle out of my arms.

When Betty's done eating, she looks much better than how we found her about half an hour ago.

"What happened, Mum?" Hans is on the verge of tears but he is trying very hard to not cry. I am worried myself. Betty looked very sickly about half an hour ago. Something must have happened to her.

"She came. She did this to me." Betty looks at the door.

"Who?" we both ask in unison.

"Her. She wore a black dress and a white collar around her neck. She tried to hurt me, Hans. She wanted to kill me," Betty frantically holds Hans's hands and is shaking like a leaf. She looks terrified, absolutely terrified of something.

"Who? Mum, did someone break into the house?"

Betty looks at Hans as if he is a ghost himself and then turns to me, "You. You must run away. She is after you."

I hate that I know who she is talking about. But how? Did Isabella try to hurt her? But why? I thought Isabella isn't capable of hurting anyone. I thought all those stories of her doing horrible things were fake. But now I am not sure anymore.

"Mom, you should sleep. Don't worry about it," Hans tells her. He has no idea what she's talking about and I pretend that I don't either.

"Please don't leave me alone, Hans. She promised she'd come again. She wants to kill me because I haven't done what she asked me to do."

"Mum, calm down. Just sleep."

Betty is mumbling something but she agrees to lie down and close her eyes. Hans tucks her in the blanket and then switches off the light. We both leave the room, deciding to give Betty some much-needed rest. Olive perches on Betty's legs and refuses to move when I tell her to. Perhaps it'd be better if she stays with Betty to give her some comfort.

"Kali, I am so sorry but I don't think I should go to the Isle of Skye," Hans says once we are in the living room and we both have a cup of tea in our hands.

"Oh, don't worry. I totally understand. You should stay with your mother. I should leave you two alone." Almost half the day has already passed and it'd be evening by the time we reach there. Besides, neither of us would feel comfortable leaving Betty behind while she's feeling so poorly. She's not my mother but I still have a lot of respect for her. I want to be by her side until I've made sure that she's feeling okay.

"I should head back home and give you two your privacy," I tell Hans. I am not sure if this is the right thing to do but I also don't want to be a burden on both of them.

"Would it be okay if you stayed with me for a while? I don't know, I just don't want to be alone for a while," Hans says.

"Of course, Hans. You look a bit shaken up too. Do you want me to get you something?"

"I am okay. Maybe a glass of water." He holds my hand and looks into my eyes. "Thanks for being here, Kali."

This time it's me who kisses him on top of his nose. "It's fine, Hans. I won't leave you alone."

I go to the kitchen to get him a glass of water. He drinks it and then stands up. "I think I should check if there are any signs of a break-in or not." Hans goes around the house checking for broken windows and open doors but I know he won't find anything. Isabella doesn't need any of that.

I just don't understand why she would attack Betty. Betty said she is punishing her for not doing something she asked her to do. But what could it be?

Olive leaves Betty's room and comes to me. I pick her up and hold her in my arms. It's comforting for me to bury my face in her fur. This whole incident has shaken me up too. I never thought Isabella could harm someone like this, I thought she just wanted me to join her coven. But attacking Betty won't help her do that. I need to talk to her. I need to face her and tell her to stop hurting the people I am close to. She's doing this for revenge, I am sure of that.

Hans returns after checking the house properly. "There are no signs of breaking in. I think mom just had an episode, I think she imagined everything."

I nod, not knowing what to say. I need to find what Isabella wants from me, I need to finally face her.

Hans gets up again. "I should call my friends and let them know we are not coming. They'd be disappointed."

"It's fine, Hans. It's not your fault. Being with your mother right now is more important than going on a holiday."

Once Hans is done with his call, he hugs me. "I know this might be too much to ask but would it be okay if I asked you to stay here with me tonight? You already have your stuff and so does Olive. I just... I just want you here right now."

"No problem, Hans. I am right here." I am more than glad to stay here tonight. I don't want to spend the night alone at my house.

Hans and I spend the rest of the day watching Netflix and playing with Olive. While playing with her, he seems relaxed. After an hour or two, we hear Betty calling for us from her bedroom.

"Do you need anything, Mum?" Hans asks as he peeks into Betty's bedroom.

"A glass of water, please."

I hand it to her and then she smiles at me. "I didn't know you were here too, Kali. And Olive too!" Olive jumps into Betty's arms and puts her head on her shoulder as Betty rubs her back.

"Mom, you seem to be in your senses now. What happened last night or early morning or whenever this happened to you?"

"Oh, I was just clumsy and I slipped. I thought I lost consciousness for a while."

"A few hours ago you said that someone was trying to hurt you," Hans says while holding his mother's hand. I am very touched by how close Hans and Betty are to each other. I wish I had such a relationship with my mother.

"Did I say that?" She looks confused but I am not sure if she really does not remember or she is pretending to not remember. If she's pretending, then she's a really good actress. She actually looks as if she's confused and trying hard to remember.

"You don't remember, Mum?"

"I don't remember anything, Hans. I do remember falling down last night from the stairs though and you coming to wake me up this morning."

"Last night? You were on the floor the whole night?" I ask.

"I am not sure anymore, Kali. I think I woke up in the middle of the night to go to the toilet. I must have slipped then."

Hans looks at me as if to ask me what we should do now. "I think Betty just needs to relax," I tell him.

"You're right," she says. "And now that I have Olive with me, I am already feeling so much better. And hungry too. Hans, can you please order something delicious for me? I am in the mood to eat some Chinese." She smacks her lips and Hans chuckles.

"Sure, I'll order something nice for you."

While Hans is ordering food, I am left wondering about what just happened. Betty doesn't remember anything she said about a few hours ago. Oh, Isabella, what game are you playing?

***

"I know this might sound awkward but would you be comfortable sleeping in this house tonight?" Hans asks me as I change into my pyjamas and we are getting ready for bed.

"What do you mean? Of course, I'd be comfortable here."

"There is a guest bedroom where you can sleep or you can sleep in the same bed as me. Choose whatever that makes you comfortable," he says with a sheepish grin on his face. I like how he is feeling shy but he is also asking for my permission.

"Um, I'd like to sleep with you if you are okay with that."

"I'd love that."

Betty is in her room sleeping peacefully. She is completely fine and it doesn't even feel like we found her unconscious on the floor just this morning. She watched TV with us throughout the day before retiring to her bedroom. Hans ordered some noodles for us for dinner and now we are going to bed. It seems that everything is okay now. But there's an uneasy feeling inside of me that makes me think otherwise.

Hans's bedroom is upstairs. I change into my pyjamas and I'm ready to go to bed. His bedroom is covered with various things. Band photos, Warhammer miniatures and there's a section of the wall covered in photos of his childhood. Each of them makes me smile wide. He was a cute kid.

"You used to be chubby," I say while pointing to a photo. Olive is lying on top of him as he's scrolling through his phone.

"Those photos are embarrassing, stop looking at them." He laughs.

"Absolutely not. In fact, I'd like to see more. Do you have an album or something?"

"What would I get if I show you my pictures?" he asks.

"What do you want?"

He shrugs. "A kiss."

I walk to him and kiss him on his lips. "You sold out just for a kiss? Pathetic. Now show me some pictures." He puts Olive aside and gets a fat album out of his cupboard.

"Here. The big book of Hans. Admire me as much as you want," he says.

The photos in this album are even cuter than the ones Hans has on the wall. I continue flipping the pages when he grabs me from behind.

"Come to bed and I will show you more of me." I put the album away and switch off the lights. I send Olive away from the bedroom because I don't want her to see us like that. She's like my child and a child should never see her mother doing this.

About an hour later, I bring her back into the room and she growls at me. I laugh and kiss her on her whiskers.

"You really love her, don't you?" Hans asks as he sees me playing around with Olive.

I lie next to him and keep my head on his shoulder. "She changed my life in the best way possible. I think she has brought good luck into my life. I was alone when I came to the city but with her by my side, I don't feel so alone anymore."

"I am surprised you say that because most people consider black cats as symbols of evil."

"No, I am not superstitious in those matters. My mum believes that Olive is evil but just look at her face, do you think she can hurt anyone at all?"

Olive perks up her ears, completely understanding that we are talking about her but still pretending that she doesn't care about what we are saying. She is such a drama queen.

"Is she going to sleep between us?"

"Nah, I don't think she will. She likes her own personal space when she comes to a new place. Although while I am alone in bed, she usually likes to sleep next to me."

Hans switches off the lights and we both are lulled to sleep. Even though today was a stressful day because of Betty's condition, I am glad the day has ended well. I fall asleep but I wake up in the middle of the light. I check the time on my phone and it's 3 a.m. Ugh. Why does this always happen to me? I always struggle with sleeping uninterrupted in a new place. I turn my phone's torchlight on to see where Olive is and I can't find her in Hans's bedroom. Strange.

I come outside to see where she is and I find her in the living room sitting on top of Hans's photo album. How did the photo album get here? I saw Hans keeping it on the table when I was done looking through it. Olive looks at me and meows. I turn on the lamp and sit next to her.

"You can't sleep at new places too, huh?" I take her in my arms and start rubbing her back, she likes it when I do that. Absent-mindedly, I open Hans's photo album once again. I see pictures of him in his school uniform, pictures of him with a Christmas tree and then pictures of him with young Betty. Betty was a mesmerisingly beautiful woman in her youth. Even today she is fit and loves to maintain her lifestyle. Just like Olive, I am glad they are in my life, both of them.

I continue turning over the pages and there are no more photos of Hans, just photos of young Betty. There's a photo of her in her wedding dress and she looks beautiful in it. I flip the page and see her sitting together with a group of young women in a circle. It looks like the pictures of her women's book club that she told me about the first day we met. It's hard to see anyone else's face except for three women sitting facing the camera. One of them is Betty and the second one... Where have I seen her before? I am sure I have seen her before. This is strange. I look closer and see all three women wearing necklaces with the pendant in the shape of the eye. It's the same necklace that I have.

And then it hits me. The woman sitting next to Betty is Ruth, Courtney's grandmother. They knew each other? I turn the page to see if there are more such photos and there are. This time the women are not sitting within a circle but instead are standing next to each other in groups of two and three. It doesn't take me too long to recognise her. Deep within my heart, I already knew I'd find her picture in this album.

Isabella Gowdie.

She is wearing the same black gown and a white collar around her neck. She is not wearing the necklace with the eye-shaped pendant. Why? I go back to the page where these women were sitting in a circle. I count them. One, two, three... there are twelve women sitting in the circle along with Isabella who has her back towards the camera. I know it's her because I see the white collar around her neck and the black dress. My heart hammers through my chest as I come to the realisation of what I am looking at.

This is Isabella's coven.

I shut the album and I notice that I am breathing hard. There are drops of sweat on my forehead. "What is happening?" I ask Olive, my only source of comfort. I do not expect a response but I hear a voice. A whisper, it could be something I am imagining or it could be true. The voice is saying my name. Again and again.

I turn around and see her standing before me, a strange smile on her face. Isabella. Her dress is torn apart and the white collar is dirty to the point of no longer being white. Her hair is bushy and her eyeliner is smudged all over her face making it seem that she is shedding black tears. She looks very different from how I saw her a few days ago in the pub. Although she's wearing the exact same outfit, it's just a lot dirtier than last time. I try to scream but my voice is stuck in my throat. I am frozen, I try to move my hands and legs to run away from her but I can't.

"Don't be afraid of me," she says. Olive is growling at her and she laughs. "This black cat is adorable, don't you think? What have you named her? Olive? Cute."

I open my mouth to say something but nothing comes out. Isabella comes around and sits next to me. As she sits next to me, I realise how much we look alike. We are roughly the same height as well as the same build. She was around my age when she passed away and she doesn't look a day older than the first picture I saw of her. We even have the same hair length.

"I know I have scared you but that was not my intention. I just want to thank you. I will even let you talk if you promise not to scream," she says calmly. Her voice is soothing, as if she is singing me a lullaby. It hits me that I am not scared of her. I am just curious and nervous.

I nod. I can't believe I am sitting next to a witch right now. I don't know if she's dangerous or not but either way, I'd like to be careful.

She snaps her fingers and it feels like I can breathe again. "You can talk now," she says.

I clear my throat and speak, "Isabella."

"Nice to finally meet you, Kali."

"What do you want from me?"

"Have I not made this clear to you already? I want to thank you, I want to thank you for what you've done."

"I didn't save you. I only freed you by accident." Surely she must know that. I never wanted to free her. I didn't even know what I was doing.

"Nothing is an accident, Kali. Anyway, I am glad you set me free, whether you did it by accident or not."

"Okay." There's a silence between us because I don't know what to say and she probably has too many things to say. We are sitting together in silence as if we are two old friends, sitting together and reminiscing memories from the past. Olive sits on the table and is looking at both of us intently. She seems like she is very much interested in this conversation. She's usually either extremely friendly with strangers or extremely hostile. But with Isabella, she's neither. She sits calmly while observing everything around her.

A moment passes before Isabella turns to me. "You should come join me, join my coven. Once you are with me, you can get whatever you want in life. It'll be fun."

I want to say no, I really want to but I can't find the words.

"Kali, you can talk now. I want to hear your answer," she says when I don't respond.

"Isabella, up until a few weeks ago, I didn't even know what a coven is. And now you want me to agree to something I know nothing about. Thanks for the offer but I politely decline. I am very happy with my life, Isabella. You must find someone else for your coven."

"What do you want to know?" she asks. She's being very patient with me, as if she's a teacher who wants to teach her student everything that she knows.

"Well, are you a witch, as people say you are?"

"I am a witch, yes you can say that. But Kali, I hope you realise that witches aren't like what people think they are." She looks at me. "What do you think being a witch would mean?"

I shrug. "I don't know. Reading tarot cards and cursing people?"

She laughs, a loud laugh that should wake everyone in this house. "Well, you can do that, if you want. But to me, being a witch means claiming my inner strength and being one with the universe." She pauses. "I grew up in a very strict household and was taught repeatedly that witches and homosexuals should be killed. Everyone who doesn't conform to the rules of society should be shunned from it. I grew up and chose to be a witch because I choose to focus on love and who I am truly supposed to be. I wonder and stay curious. It is how I explore the unknown, whatever that means for me at the moment." She looks at me and then smiles. "Being a witch means recognising and honouring that I am a being who is no longer allowing her repression. And I want other women to feel this way too."

I won't lie, Isabella's definition of being a witch resonates with me. "That does sound very nice, Isabella." This seems to make her happy. "Are you alive?" I ask a question which may seem stupid but it's something I am very serious about.

"I am both alive and dead. They tried to kill me but they couldn't. But I punished them. I punished them by killing them."

A chill runs down my spine. She's killed people before. A good witch wouldn't do that. I understand that she doesn't want to be repressed but killing other people is not something I can support. "Isabella, I think I am okay being who I am."

She doesn't speak for a moment and I am scared I've angered her. But then she responds, "I just don't understand why you would choose a simple life rather than a life full of magic and miracles."

"I... I don't know. I like how simple things are in my life."

She laughs and then gets up. Perhaps she is leaving right now since I have told her I do not want to join her coven. But she turns around and then looks at me with no hint of a smile on her face. "You will regret this." She waves her hand and disappears. I release a breath that I did not know I was holding. At least she is gone now and hopefully won't be back soon.

I go back to Hans's bedroom and close my eyes. I just don't understand why she's so fixated on me. I am just a simple girl. Now that I am thinking about it, I would like to be a witch but I don't want to join her coven. Although I do wonder what I am going to write in my research now. My research was all about how innocent women were implicated as witches for crimes they did not commit but I can't say the same about Isabella. Now I feel stupid. I should have taken my notebook out and asked her all the questions that I needed to ask for my research. But I was too dumbstruck, at least I had Olive by my side.

Olive!

Where is she now? I get up from the bed and run to the living room but she is not there on the sofa. Instead, there's a torn page lying on top of it. It's Isabella's handwriting, I recognise it from her diary. They are the same words she said before disappearing. *You are going to regret this.*

Chapter 7

Olive is gone. Isabella must have taken her. She took my cat away because I refused to leave everything in my life to join her coven. Does she think this would make me run back to her and accept her offer? I don't think so. But I do need to get Olive back somehow.

Hans finds me in the morning crying with Isabella's letter clutched in my hands.

"Oh my god, Kali. What happened? Why are you crying?" He looks worried, it's the same expression I saw on his face just yesterday when he found his mother lying on the floor.

I shake my head at him and wipe my tears. I can't break down right now, I need to get my cat back. I hear footsteps approaching and for a moment I think Isabella's back but it's only Betty.

"Oh, dear. Is everything okay?" She looks at Hans and then at me.

"I am okay, Betty. Although I do have some questions for you." I have a lot of things that I need to ask Betty. Betty has a role in all of this and I'd like to know what exactly it is.

"Questions for me? Ask away, Kali. You know you can ask me anything." She sits next to me.

I look around and find the album toppled on the floor. I pick it up. "What is this, Betty?" I point to her photo with Isabella.

Betty looks at Hans as if I am totally out of my mind. "Where did you find this?"

"Does it matter? Just tell me what this is."

"It's a club I am a part of. I told you. We meet once every month and..."

"This is a photo of your coven and you meet every full moon. Am I right?"

Betty doesn't respond and looks at Hans.

"Kali, what are you blabbering about?" Hans asks.

I turn to him. "Hans, I saw her last night. I saw the woman who attacked your mother just a day before."

"I slipped and fell on the floor, Kali. I told you." I look at Betty in disbelief. She's lying. But why? Why is she trying to protect Isabella?

"Alright, whatever. But what is happening in this picture? Who are these women?" I ask again.

Hans responds before Betty can. "Don't you think you are being a bit intrusive right now, Kali?"

I close my eyes trying not to lose my patience. I open them again and look at Betty waiting for her to say something but she continues to stare at me with her mouth open. She finally responds, "That's my book club. We meet every month to discuss the books we've read. We are not a coven. How marvellous would that be if we were though." She nervously laughs.

I hold my head in hand. I am not going to get any help here. "Hans, I think I should go back home. I just don't feel very good." I realise that Betty won't answer any of my questions, not while Hans is here.

"Alright, I'll drop you." He stands up.

"No, no. I'll take an Uber. You stay here."

Right now I just want to be alone. I don't want anyone around me, not even Hans. Besides, I dislike how he called me intrusive for asking his mother a few questions. These are important questions and I am going to find the answer to them, whether Betty talks or not.

I call an Uber and collect my luggage. I take my suitcase and Olive's empty cage and her litter box.

"Where's Olive?" Hans asks.

"She's gone," I say before getting in the car.

***

I need to find out what happened with Isabella as soon as possible. She's dangerous and when she doesn't get what she wants, she attacks people. She isn't some innocent woman who was vilified for her sexuality. She is truly a witch, a bad one. And her actions are hurting witches who aren't evil.

Even though it's Sunday, I spend the day researching when I come back to my flat. I come back to an empty flat as my mother is not home. I have no idea where she's gone again but I don't have time to be worried about her right now. Besides, I am thankful for the peace and quiet in the house. She'd have so many questions for me otherwise. She'd even celebrate a little if she finds out Olive is gone. She hated my poor cat.

I lock myself in my bedroom and spend the day researching Isabella even though it's a Sunday and I am not supposed to work today. Finding everything about Isabella is more than my job now, it has seeped into my personal life. I go back to the document that Henry shared with me on the very first day of my job. It mentions everything that is known about Isabella publicly. She was convicted for the murder of three women, women who saw her practising her black magic. Now I wonder if she killed them because they saw her or because she asked them to join her coven and they refused. If the latter's the case, I might even be in danger. Isabella kills whoever she wants and doesn't even feel guilty. I understand that she was treated poorly but that doesn't mean she can go on a killing spree and murder anyone who doesn't do what she asks them to do.

But I don't want to worry about my life right now. I have starved for love my whole life. My parents weren't there for me and I didn't have many close friends while growing up. Olive was the first person, an animal who loved me back without expecting anything in return. She taught me unconditional love. I don't know where she is right now, if she's still even alive. But I want to get her back. I don't even know if she's safe or not. That's the only thing I care about right now.

But how do I find her? Where do I even begin my search? I need to find Isabella and not only find her but also get my cat back.

I am reminded of Isabella's diary I found weeks ago and start to read it again hoping I'd find something useful.

21st September

Annabeth got me flowers today. They were bright, red roses. She said, "They were perfect flowers for a woman like me!" I think she fancies me, I fancy her too. Marianne told me she keeps asking about me all the time when I am not around. My little sister is starting to get jealous but she doesn't understand that our friendship is of a different kind. Sometimes I think I must control my thoughts, the way I feel about another woman is not natural after all. But then I look at Annabeth and I realise I can't control how I feel about her even if I force myself to. I don't know what to do anymore. Mumma has been forcing me to talk to Mr Richard who lives next door. She wants me to marry him but I just can't. I don't know what I am going to do.

1st December

Marianne came to our house today and gave me the most shocking news. She informed me that Annabeth got married in London to a man her father thought was suitable for her. I had to pretend to smile and act happy in front of Marianne but how could Annabeth do this to me? We've spent the last few months together almost every day meeting each other. She even kissed me on my forehead the other day making me believe she feels the same way about me as I feel for her. I don't know if it is possible for us to be together but nonetheless, we both had agreed to never marry and be friends forever. And now she has betrayed me like this...

10th January

I can't go on, the pain of losing Annabeth is too much to bear. Yesterday, Marianne told me Annabeth is back from London with her husband. They invited both of us to tea in the evening. I didn't want to go at all but Marianne said I should go, for the sake of Annabeth. I forced myself to get up and Marianne helped me dress up. I don't know how women without sisters survive. I couldn't stop my tears but at least I had Marianne to give me some comfort. Suffering from love is the worst disease on earth.

At tea, I stayed silent while everyone else around me continued talking. Annabeth's husband is handsome and very rich. Of course, she chose to marry him. Oh, my agony. My life is ruined. Annabeth hugged me as soon as she saw me. She pretended as if nothing had changed. She seemed happy, as if she willingly chose to marry this man. It seems as if she doesn't even remember the numerous days we spent with each other.

31st January

The last few months of my life have been painful. I wake up every day with tears in my eyes and I go to bed with tears in my eyes too. Life is not fair. I was by the river last week crying my heart out when a kind woman approached me. She spent the whole afternoon with me and told me about a club for women, a club that helps women get through the pain. I am going to attend the club meeting this weekend. Hopefully, I will feel better.

12 February

The club met outside Tantallon Castle by the North Sea. I didn't know what to expect when I went there but the women were all friendly and made me feel comfortable. I told them about my problems and they gave me comfort with their words. We sat together in a circle and prayed to the full moon. The women comforted me in these dark times. I think I will join their club.

22nd March

The women's club has some peculiar rituals. Rituals I am not sure my mother would approve of. The women made me draw a small effigy of Annabeth's husband from the clay. They said I should treat the effigy as if it is George himself. They told me I could hurt George whenever I wanted. The idea is interesting to me, I do admit but I haven't tried *anything yet. I am going to visit George and Annabeth tomorrow and see if what the women said was true or not. Oh if I could hurt George!*

23rd March

I can't believe that the trick worked! Before heading out today in the afternoon, I cut the effigy's little finger and threw it in the fire. I didn't think anything would really happen but when I went to meet George and Annabeth, I saw that George's hand got burnt when he was lighting the chimney fire. I felt better, so much better. It means that the spell I was taught by those women worked. I am going to back to those women and learn some more spells.

31st April

I have found happiness. I never thought I would find happiness again but the other women in the club have made me see the path of light. I have power now. I have magic. I can do whatever I want, and take whatever should belong to me. Like fire burns, so do my enemies. I feel like I am born again and the whole world is in the palm of my hands.

There are no more entries after this. I wish Isabella wrote more in her diary. She wrote sporadically and whenever she did, she only wrote a few lines. The rituals, the magic, I almost don't want to believe in them but I do. Isabella won't lie in her diary. I feel sad about what happened to her but at the same time, I can see that she'd do anything to hurt those who hurt her. She feels as if the world owes her everything but it doesn't.

But at least I know where I have to begin my search now. Tantallon Castle. This is the place that was mentioned in her diary and I am sure I'd find something once I go there. It's worth checking out. Who knows what I'd find there?

A quick Google research tells me this castle is in North Berwick, about an hour and a half away from Glasgow by train. I look outside my window and see the setting sun. It's already evening right now, it'll be dark by the time I reach there. I must wait until tomorrow.

I put my laptop away and sigh. No. I don't care if it gets dark by the time I reach there, I need to go there right now. I won't be able to sleep peacefully tonight anyway. I take my keys and leave. To go to Berwick, I need to go to Edinburgh and then change my train there. While I am on the train, I keep overthinking what might happen to Olive. How did I even get entangled in this mess? About a few weeks ago, I didn't even have a cat and look at me now. I am going after a witch in the dark to bring my cat back.

I quickly Google North Berwick on my phone to see what kind of town it is. Google tells me it's a seaside town famous for its beach. The castle is on the beach as well. I do love beaches but I don't think I've ever been to a beach in the dark. I usually like them when it's sunny and I have a glass of vodka in my hands. I take a deep breath. I don't know what I'll find at the castle. Will I find Isabella? Perhaps. Will I find her coven? I don't know.

As I am looking outside the window, I remember Henry telling me something about North Berwick. It is exactly here where the earliest Scottish witches were found. They were trying to capsize King James VI's boat. Witch trials were held here and several witches were burned. I am excited as well as scared about what I might end up finding there.

By the time I come outside the North Berwick train station, it's pitch dark outside. The station is only illuminated by a few lamps. No one gets off the train with me. Obviously, no one comes to the beach at night, except people who live in this town. I can smell the sea breeze as soon I step outside.

I take my phone out and put down Tantallon castle's location. It's a forty-minute walk away. On the way, I don't find many street lights so I am walking in the dark with only the dim light from the moon. I look up and see a full moon shining above my head. I remember on the last full moon I was with Courtney participating in witch rituals and tonight I am going after a coven. Wow. I'd rather be doing those rituals than walking alone to a beach in the dark.

I do not come across anyone as I am walking to the beach. It's a very small town and most people are indoors right now. When I see the castle in the distance, I take a deep breath. I didn't think much before leaving the house and coming here. I just wanted to save my cat but now with the dark, scary castle standing before me, I feel numb. A few more steps and I am there.

I see the silhouette of the castle against the night sky. It looks haunting and now that I am here, I feel scared. I do not go inside the castle. I stand outside waiting to accumulate enough strength when I notice something drawn on the sand. A circle with an eye in between. Isabella must have been here. Or someone from her coven. I think this symbol belongs to the coven. I walk a little further and then I see some names written on the wall of the castle with a red liquid which I assume is blood. I count the names. There are twelve of them. It seems these names are of the women who are in the coven.

Isabella wants me to join her coven. She wants my name on the wall along with these women. But I will never be that woman. I will never agree to give up everything for a little bit of magic. I am not like Isabella. I do not hurt people simply because I don't like them.

I am still reading the names when I hear a sound. I turn around and see someone walking towards me in the distance. I stoop down on the floor and grab a big rock. I don't know if I can hurt whoever it is with this tiny rock but I sure am not going to give up without putting up a fight. The figure continues walking towards me and I notice it's a woman. It's not Isabella, I can tell that much. When the woman is only a few steps away, I finally see who it is. It's my mother.

"Mom?" I go closer to her but she doesn't notice that it's me. She looks like a walking corpse. "Mom, are you alright?" I ask but she doesn't reply. Her eyes are open but she is not looking at me. I hold her by her waist trying to wake her up but nothing works on her. She looks like she is under a spell.

I need to take her away from here. I hold her and drag her back to the train station. The forty-minute walk away takes me well over an hour because Mom is walking way too slowly. By the time I reach there, the cafe is closed. I sit on a bench along with my mother and try to shake her. She doesn't wake up. What am I going to do now? First my cat and now my mother.

I check if there's anything helpful in my bag and thankfully I find a small bottle of water. I sprinkle a few drops on her face and she suddenly wakes up, really wakes up.

"Kali?" She is confused, she has no idea where she is and how she has got here, it seems.

"Mom, are you okay?"

She peels herself away from me. "I am fine, what are you doing here? How did I get here?"

"I'd like to ask you the same thing. What are you doing here on this beach?"

She doesn't answer my question. "Kali, I feel too weak. Can you please take me back home?" She puts her arm around my shoulder and I drag her inside the train station. I buy another ticket for her and we head back home.

She is too weak on the train and I don't ask her anything just now. This has to be Isabella's work. How else would my mother come here on the beach by herself in the dark? But why is she here in the first place? She was supposed to be with her friend.

By the time we reach home, it's almost midnight. I quickly heat some soup to feed my mother and she falls asleep soon after. Since my bedroom is right by the entrance, I take her into my bedroom rather than hers. I change into my pyjamas and lie next to her.

Years must have passed since the last time I lay next to her. I feel conflicting emotions brewing inside of me. On one hand, it's comforting. She's my mother and all I have ever wanted from her is her love but on the other hand, it feels awful. She never gave me the love that I craved so much from her. But she expects everything from me now that I've grown up. She's gone from being an abusive mother to a needy one. I had to save her today. What was she doing near the castle?

The lights are still switched on and I lie awake thinking about what I am going to do now. Perhaps my mother will have some answers for me when she wakes up. I might have to go back to the castle again and actually go inside. There's witchcraft happening in North Berwick. I have a feeling that I might find all my answers there.

I Google again since I can't fall asleep. I have a few unread messages from Hans asking if I am okay. I will respond to him tomorrow. He must be so confused with how I have been acting. It's not his fault, I am confused too. There is a museum in Berwick, an art museum. I don't know if I'll find anything there but it's worth a visit. Museums usually have old snippets of history and maybe they have something about witches.

I put my phone away and turn off the lights. I need to sleep if I want to wake up early tomorrow and go back there. I close my eyes and drift off to sleep. I toss and turn around because I wake up after every few minutes hoping I'd find Olive sleeping next to me but I don't. It's a very disturbing night for me.

I am dreaming of something when I feel something around my neck. In my dream, it seems to be Isabella's white collar tightening around my neck trying to suffocate me but when I open my eyes, my mother's hands are wrapped around my neck. She is trying to strangle me. I use my hands to push her away but she is too strong for me. She is acting like she was acting when I found her on the beach, like a dead corpse. She is not herself.

Her grip around my throat tightens as I move around to free myself from her. She is strong, too strong for me and for a moment I see darkness. It is the end but then I find an unexplained surge of energy within me and I push her away.

"STAY AWAY FROM ME." My voice is loud and I don't recognise myself when I scream. However, my voice does the trick and my mom is awake again.

"Kali, why are you screaming at me?" she asks as she falls on the floor.

"Screaming at you? You just tried to kill me!"

"What are you talking about? Why are you always blaming me for things I didn't do?" She looks around as if she has no idea where she is.

I get up and stare at my mother. I usually let her say whatever she wants to say to me but I can't control my anger anymore. "Your hands were around my neck. You were a moment away from killing me."

She looks scandalised as if I am framing her for a crime she didn't do. I take a deep breath. It is right. She didn't know what she was doing. It wasn't her fault. But that doesn't mean I am not angry at her.

"I am sorry, Mom. I didn't mean to yell."

"Kali, I can't believe you. You always treat me like your worst enemy." There are tears in her eyes and I know she is being melodramatic right now. That's how she manipulates me every time.

"Mom, you said that you were going to spend the weekend with your friend. Tell me who this friend is."

"Her name is… Oh my god, Kali. I can't remember what it is. But why do you ask?"

I don't have the patience to fight with her right now. "Do you have any photos with her? You love taking pictures with your friends."

She searches for her phone kept in her jeans pocket and hands it to me. I go to her gallery but all the photos in the gallery are of her alone. There is no one along with her. I show her the photos. "There's no one with you in these photos."

She takes the phone from me and looks at it in disbelief. "How can this be? She was with me. In all of these photos."

"Do you remember what she looks like?" I ask impatiently. Either my mother is lying to me or she is mentally sick or maybe Isabella is behind all of this. I don't know which of these outcomes is worse.

"Well, she has long black hair and she loves wearing black dresses. And she always wore something around her neck, it's like a round white scarf."

I close my eyes. Isabella. She has been hanging out with my mother all this while. Was this another one of her traps laid out for me?

"Mom, it's fine. You need to rest." There's no point in blaming my mother for things she doesn't remember doing. But now the question is what has Isabella been making my mother do all this while? She befriended her for a reason but what is it? My mom could still be under her spell right now, my mother can attack me once again unconsciously. It's not safe for me to be around her. But I need help. I don't know anything about witchcraft, I never took it seriously. But thankfully I know someone who does.

***

Courtney is surprised to see me when I arrive at her door at 9 a.m. in the morning. Her dog Zeus doesn't bark at me this time perhaps because he has recognised me. He sniffs my hand and wags his tail playfully.

"What is it, Kali? You look absolutely horrible," Courtney says as she lets me in.

"I feel horrible. But you can help me. I am sorry to disturb you and coming here without telling you. But it's a little bit urgent. Are you free right now?"

"Uhh... yeah."

I tell her everything from the very beginning, everything that has happened to me since I moved to Glasgow. Finding Olive, Isabella, the night at the Tantallon castle where I found my mother. It takes me a while to finish my story. So much has happened and it's difficult for me to put everything together coherently. She listens to me attentively with her mouth slightly open and when I finish, she doesn't seem as astonished as I expected her to be.

"So, what is going on?" I ask once I am finished talking.

Courtney is silent for a long time, it feels as if she'll never speak again but then she does. "Isabella is an evil witch, she doesn't practise magic like other witches do." Now I feel horrible for thinking less of Courtney while she was doing her law of manifestation techniques. Making wishes on paper is much better than stealing cats and murdering people.

"What do I do now? I am scared to be around my own mother. Don't you know of anything that would break this spell? There has to be something."

She thinks for a moment. "I can't think of anything right now but you know what? Come with me."

She stands up abruptly and asks me to follow her. "What are you doing?" I ask her as she is looking deep within her cupboard throwing all her clothes away. She takes out a box and shows it to me.

"We might find something here."

"What is this?"

"This is my grandmother's stuff that was passed down to my mother. But I don't think she ever looked into it. It was too painful for her."

"Where is your mother now?"

"She passed away."

"Oh, I am sorry."

"Don't worry about it. Come, let's look inside."

We sit on her carpeted floor and open the box. There are all sorts of weird things inside. Burnt candles, old love letters and books, some charms and even the necklace with the eye pendant. We both look through the stuff to find something useful when I spot a small diary underneath everything. It looks very similar to Isabella's diary. I open it and recognise her handwriting at once.

"This is Isabella's diary," I tell Courtney.

"Oh my god. Open it."

And together we begin to read.

Isabella

I am not a witch. Well, not the kind of witch that hexes people. I can do some tricks and I can make children laugh. I once changed a mouse into a bunny and a bunny into a pigeon. Sometimes I still can't believe I can do these things.

When I went to my first meeting at the women's club, I didn't know what to expect. I was just looking for some company after I got my heart broken. But over the years, they have accepted me in a way that no one ever has. We formally meet once a month at the full moon but informally we meet each other every week.

We are the best of friends now. We share our sorrows and happiness. I cannot believe my life without these women. When they showed me that I could mend my broken heart with magic, I couldn't believe them. I thought they were joking! But then Agnes put her hands on me and my pain was gone in an instant.

No, it wasn't really gone. It changed into a rage. I wanted revenge on Annabeth. Agnes helped me make a George-shaped doll and after burning his hand, I went on to torture him slowly. I could have killed him in an instant, that's what all the other witches suggested I should have done but I wanted to hurt Annabeth more, I wanted her to be in as much pain as she put me through. I hurt George first and when I got bored, I started hurting Annabeth. She deserved the pain. She deserved worse than what I did to her. I first disfigured her face. If I couldn't see that beautiful face every day, then no one ever should. And then I made her infertile. She wanted to be a mother but I wasn't going to let her have that happiness. I could see how much she was in love with George. The way she looked at George, she never looked at me that way. I realised that she never loved me like she loved George. So I took George from her. I killed him. And when I went to see her at his funeral, I was truly happy.

My coven made it possible for me. It was thanks to my sister that I finally got my revenge. When Agnes, the leader of our coven, was about to sacrifice herself to the fire and leave this world for good, she asked me to take her place. Everyone else in the coven was happy with her decision. Except for Julie. So, Agnes burnt Julie along with her.

But now I have to find another witch for the coven, another powerful witch. Where do I even begin my search? I had stayed in the coven long enough to know what kind of women we usually looked for. Lonesome women who were tired of their lives but no, I need someone else. Someone stronger, someone who is like me.

I have considered several women for this position, but none of them proved to be strong enough for the coven. While it is my duty to look for the thirteenth witch, the entire coven has to approve of her. I don't know how I'll find her.

***

I think I have found the thirteenth witch. She is only fifteen years old, her name is Dierdre. She comes and plays around my hut every day, she is interested in me, interested in what I might have inside the hut. It's possible she has heard the voices, it might even be possible she saw the coven on the full moon in the woods sacrificing our victims. I am interested in seeing if she can pass the test.

**

My test for whether a woman is worthy to be a witch or not is simple. I put a cat near her house. I want a witch who takes care of poor souls. Black cats are intuitive animals, they can sense magic and are only drawn to girls who have it in themselves to be a witch. Deirdre didn't pay attention to the black cat at first but then she took the bait. She took her inside but perhaps her mother said no to keeping the cat. Nonetheless, she fed the cat every day in secret.

My next step was to give her the necklace with the pendant in the shape of the eye. It's an old symbol of witchcraft. The eye can See, the eye can test. I left the necklace as a Christmas present outside her door and saw her wearing it later that week. If Dierdre wasn't worthy enough to be a witch, the necklace would have strangled her. But it didn't.

I took a few more tests to make sure she was the right one. I placed the eggs in her kitchen and they broke, pouring blood out. If there wasn't any blood, it would have been a sign that she wasn't ready to be a witch. It is time for me to present myself to her now. She has passed all my tests and now she deserves a reward. She needs to join the coven. And if she doesn't, I'll have to kill her.

***

Deirdre said no. How could she? I took the cat away from her and hypnotised her mother to kill her. She has seen too much now and if she doesn't want to join our coven anymore, the only alternative is death.

The notebook is blank after this. I look at Courtney.

"All of these things have happened to me, Courtney. I think she is going to kill me now," I say with my heart hammering through my chest.

"Then do something. If you are dead, you can't save your mother and your cat."

"I don't think Olive needs to be saved now. She was never mine, she was always hers." The realisation hurts me deeply. I thought Olive had grown to love me but she was just an animal who enjoyed being fed regularly. I didn't know it was even possible to be heartbroken over a cat but here I am. My mother's words echo in my head, she always wanted me to get rid of Olive. Perhaps I should have.

"I think Olive still loved you, she is just an animal and Isabella probably manipulated her."

"Yeah, maybe. But none of this helps me. I need to know more. How do I break a spell? And since I have already passed all of Isabella's tests, am I witch now?"

"No, that's not how it works. You can't become a witch until you truly want to. That's something I know for sure."

I take a deep breath and lie down on the floor. I am exhausted. "Courtney, what do I do now?"

She is still looking into the box when I ask her the question. "Look, I found something."

I stand up to see what it is. She hands me the paper and I read it. It's some kind of recipe. "What even is this, Courtney?"

"It's a spell. See, it's a spell to make love potions. Heather, honey and cat's blood. You feed it to someone and you make them fall in love with you."

"Wow, that's gross. I don't think I want a man in my life if I don't have his consent."

She takes out more letters from the box. They are all spells. Spell to make an animal turn into a bird, spell to make someone jealous of you, spell to avenge your enemy. I have to admit that it's all very fascinating. "None of these spells would be useful for me. I need to break my mother's spell, not make her fall in love with me using a love potion."

"Kali, I know what you need to do."

She gets up and takes a big box out of her cupboard. It's her Ouija board. "Who are we going to call?"

"My grandmother."

It's the middle of the day so neither of us is sure if Grandma Ruth would appear but Courtney switches off the lights and burns some candles.

"What are you going to ask her?" I ask Courtney but she doesn't respond. "You'll see."

"Grandma Ruth, please come here and help us." Neither of us put our hands on the triangle like Courtney made the witches do the other night and yet the triangle moves on 'yes.'

Courtney and I rejoice. I clear my throat and ask my question. "Hello, Grandma Ruth. I am Kali, Courtney's friend." I feel silly introducing myself to a spirit. Of course, the spirit knows who I am. I continue, "Can you teach me how to break a spell?"

We wait for the triangle to move but it doesn't. I look at Courtney. "Perhaps you should ask her this question since she's your grandmother."

She's about to say something when the triangle moves. G,O,T,O,B,E,R,W,I,C,K.

"Berwick? Why?" Courtney asks.

"I know what she is talking about. Tantallon castle. That's where I found my hypnotised mother. I think there's something happening in the castle. Witchcraft."

We say goodbye to Grandma Ruth's spirit. I finally know where I have to go. Courtney offers to come along with me but I decline. She's a good witch and I don't want to get her mixed up with dark magic any more than she already is. She has helped me a lot and I make a mental note that I need to do something to thank her as well as apologise to her for laughing at her rituals.

"I will tell you everything that I find there. But for now, I need you to stay here. I don't want to push you in danger. Besides, if something happens to me, I'll need you to do some of your rituals and come save me."

She nods. "Good luck, Kali. All you have to do is believe in yourself and you'll defeat Isabella." She's probably right. I don't know much about being a witch but I do know that I need to have faith in myself.

As soon as I am out of her building and on my way to the train station, my phone buzzes. It's Henry. I am tempted to not pick up the phone but I don't want to get into any trouble with him so I answer the call. What does he want from me?

"Where are you, Kali?" He sounds angry.

"I... I am actually researching. I found Isabella's old diary and there is something happening in Berwick. That's where I am headed."

"You do realise that I am your supervisor, right?"

I stop in my tracks. "Yes, Henry. I know you are my supervisor."

"And yet you didn't seek my permission before doing all of this."

"I am sorry but I thought you would encourage me to go to Berwick and find out what happened with Isabella."

"Do you know what day it is?"

"Uh, Monday."

"Did you forget?"

"Forget what?"

"The conference was organised by the History Department today. We all were supposed to present our research and you weren't there."

I totally forgot about that. Damn, it's only reasonable that Henry is angry at me. "I am sorry, Henry. It totally slipped my mind."

"You did this on purpose, didn't you? We lost the opportunity to secure extra funding."

"Why would I purposely reject an opportunity to get my own salary raised, Henry? What are you even talking about?"

"I want you to come to the office right now. This is a serious issue and I can't let you go so easily. The other girls would be disappointed in me if I do that."

"Henry, is this really important? Can't it wait until I get back from Berwick?"

"No, it absolutely cannot. You must come as soon as possible."

"But Henry I—"

"Come here right now or you will lose your job."

I take a deep breath. I can't lose my composure. I will quickly deal with Henry once I reach the office and then leave. It won't take much time. "Alright, Henry. I will be there in fifteen minutes."

***

Henry is sitting at his computer typing away when I reach the office. As soon as I open the door, all the eyes are on me. Esme, Natacha and Lisa look at me as if I committed a crime. I feel guilty. This conference was important to all of them, it was important to me too. But it slipped my mind.

"Hi," I meekly say. Henry looks up from his computer but doesn't smile at me.

"I need to talk to you in private. Can you girls please leave the room?" The girls leave the room quietly all while giving me angry glares. "So, Kali. Can you please tell me why you decided to take a day off today without informing me?"

"I explained to you, Henry. I found a lead that I thought I should follow in Berwick. The Tantallon castle that you told me about, there is something happening there. Isabella has got something to do with it and I just want to learn what it is."

Henry continues looking at me without saying anything. He takes a deep breath. "You are so good at lying."

"I am not lying, Henry. Why would I lie about something like this?"

"I think all of us knew that you were headed to the Isle of Skye this weekend. I think you decided to extend your holiday by adding one more day and now you've cooked up some story so you don't get into trouble."

"Henry, that's not true. I didn't go on the trip because Hans's mother got sick and we couldn't go. Isabella attacked her, Henry."

"Isabella? The witch you are doing your research on?"

"Yes. I know it sounds bizarre but please at least listen to me."

"Are you mad or do you think I have gone mad?" He stands up and comes closer to me. "Did you have a good weekend with your boyfriend? Did you fuck?" His face has completely transformed. I have seen him look like this and at this moment, I am very, very scared and I wish I wasn't alone with him in this room right now. I am appalled he'd ask me something like this. "I don't think this is important to this conversation," I say calmly even though I am not calm at all. I need to have my wits about me right now.

"Of course, it is." He holds my wrist tightly.

"Henry, leave me alone. Just because I missed a day of work doesn't mean you can harass me. I can report you to the authorities."

"Shut the fuck up." He holds me by my waist and forcefully kisses me. For a second, I am too stunned to move and then I push him away.

"Stay away from me." He stumbles and falls down on his desk, dropping his laptop. The commotion makes the girls come back into the office.

"What is happening?" Natacha says.

"He forced himself on me," I say with tears streaming down my cheeks.

Esme steps forward and helps Henry get up. "You're lying. She's lying." Henry is so good at pretending and since the girls found him on the floor rather than me, I can tell whose side they are on. Esme is the only one who is talking and the rest of the girls are staring at us silently as if they don't know what to say.

"He forced himself on you? But over the last month, you've been throwing yourself all over him. We all saw it," Esme says with anger.

"What? What are you talking about?" I can't believe they'd say something like this. Me throwing myself at him? All those lunches and drink nights were planned by him and not me.

"Oh, come on. Stop pretending like you're a saint. You were asking him to all these lunches and staying with him in bars after we left. We all saw you were constantly flirting with him and now just because you are about to lose your job, you're falsely implicating him. That's disgusting."

I can't believe how much vitriol Esme is spewing. I look at Natacha and Lisa hoping they'd say something in my favour but they don't. Understanding that I am completely alone in this situation, I take my bag and leave the room. I run to the bathroom and shut myself in a stall. I cry my heart out.

What is even happening in my life? When I moved here, I didn't think all of this would happen to me. And now I am alone. I am truly alone. Not even my cat is with me. I come outside the stall to wash my face. I splash a few drops of water on my face and then look up. Instead of seeing my own reflection in the mirror, I see Isabella.

"What are you doing here?" I am not scared at the sight of her. I am angry, angry at her for ruining my life.

"Poor Kali. I came here to give you some company." She's wearing the same black dress and white collar. But her hair is tamed. She is looking beautiful right now. It looks like she's winning and she knows that.

"Why don't you leave me alone? I don't want to join your stupid coven. I will never become what you've become," I say through my tears.

"Don't you see? If you come to our side, if you join the coven, you can do whatever you want. You can torture that little Henry, you can torture your mother for hurting you. Join us."

"Why are you so hell-bent on me joining your coven? Why don't you just kill me like you killed Dierdre?"

"How do you know about her?" she drops the fake sweet tone she was using with me and speaks in anger.

"Answer my questions and I'll tell you. Why me?"

"You set me free, Kali. Do you know how many people have tried to set me free before you came? Hundreds. I was stuck there for months and months. I used my powers to lure victims, I asked other witches to free me and they couldn't. There's something about you… You are powerful, Kali. You are even more powerful than me. I can't let go of you so easily."

It's hard to believe whatever Isabella is saying. Am I powerful? I must be. Why else would Isabella be after me with such passion? For a moment, I think about joining her coven. She is right. If I do join her coven, I can do things that I want. I can do anything that I want.

"I need some time to think," I tell her and her face splits into a wide, grotesque grin.

"Attagirl. Take your time and let me know your answer soon."

"Will my mother attack me if I go back home?"

"No, no she won't. Everything will be okay now. Your life is going to transform. Bye, Kali. Whenever you are ready to tell me your answer, just think of me. I'll inform other witches about you."

Isabella disappears leaving me staring at my own reflection. I don't know if I'll actually end up joining Isabella's coven but at least for now, she has left me alone. I have to be careful about what I do now. I have to be careful with every step I take.

Chapter 8

Even though Isabella assured me that my mother won't attack me, I don't go back to my home. The only reason I was going back to my home every day was Olive and now she's gone. It strikes me that if I do join Isabella's coven, I'll get to meet her again.

I find myself outside Hans's flat. I knock on his door but he doesn't open it. I check the time. He probably isn't back from work yet. So I take a walk along the river. It's a beautiful day today and sometimes I forget that I am surrounded by so much beauty around me. All the things that have been happening in my life have made me forget to actually enjoy my life, which is why I moved away from home in the first place.

I sit by the river on a bench waiting for Hans and half an hour later, he appears. We haven't spoken at length to each other since the last time I was with him at Betty's house.

"Hey, Kali. What are you doing here outside?" he asks as he kisses my cheek.

"I just didn't want to be alone right now. Did I come at a bad time?" I ask as I hold his hand and feel his warmth.

"Oh no. I just came back from the office and now I am going over to my mother's house. She's fine now but I still get worried. I don't like leaving her alone for long periods. You should come with me."

I don't know if I want to meet Betty. She is a witch who belongs to Isabella's coven and yet refuses to talk anything about it. She can help me a lot simply by choosing to talk to me. But she doesn't. But at the same time, I don't want to be alone right now. I guess I can forget everything for a while and go meet her. "Sure, I'd love to."

"I just gotta get changed into something more comfortable. Come inside."

Hans takes me inside. I wait for him in the living room while he changes his clothes. I look into my hands while I wait for him to come back into the room. I feel so overwhelmed right now. All I want to do is lie down and take a long nap. But I can't. I won't be able to rest easy until I solve all of the mess that is in my life.

"You look a bit worried, did something happen? Did you find Olive?" he asks. He thinks Olive simply ran away that night and I have not said anything to change his mind. His mother probably knows everything and if she hasn't told him anything, I doubt Hans would believe anything I say.

"No, not yet. Also, something happened today," I tell him everything about what happened with Henry. I also tell him the previous times when Henry tried to get close to me and tried to touch my hands or shoulders whenever he got the opportunity. In hindsight, I can see that his behaviour towards me was creepy from the very beginning. Back then, I just assumed he's the kind of person who doesn't understand the concept of personal space. But no, now I realise that he was very much aware of what he was doing. I also realise that he never behaved the way he did with me with any other girl. The worst part is that none of the girls even questioned whether he could be wrong. They blindly believed him. Perhaps because they've worked with Henry for such a long time and he never behaved that way with them. I tell Hans everything. His face contorts and I can tell that he is both angry and sad at the same time. I feel the same way too.

"You have to report him, Kali. That's sexual harassment," he says once I have finished talking. He's right. I do have to report him. I just wish I didn't have to deal with all this while I am being haunted by a witch.

"Yeah, I will. But I doubt anyone would believe me. All the girls took his side. They've worked with him for so long and he never did anything appropriate to them." I pause. "It makes me think I may have done something to lead him on."

"Kali, no. None of it is your fault. You should still report him, whether anyone believes you or not. I can't have some douche treat my girl like that." He hugs me and I break into tears once again on his shoulders. Too much is happening and I was desperately in need of a hug.

"Let's go, Hans. We don't want to be late for dinner," I tell him. I don't want to think about Henry right now. I will deal with him later. Just thinking about it is giving me a headache.

Hans drives us to Betty's flat. We stop and get some McDonald's on the way since Betty loves it. Hans also buys me a big tub of ice cream to cheer me up.

When Betty sees me at the door, she nervously smiles. "Oh, Kali. I didn't know you were coming too." I can tell that she's uncomfortable with me showing up here but is too polite to say anything. This assures me that Betty is indeed hiding something from me.

"I hope you don't mind. I just wanted to see you to make sure you are doing better than the last time I saw you," I say. She is playing it cool and so am I. There's no point in forcing her to say something in front of Hans. She just wouldn't. I am just going to pretend nothing has changed between us and we are still friends like we used to be.

She takes us inside and rejoices when she sees the food in Hans's arms.

"Oh, you are spoiling me these days, Hans. I shouldn't be eating such food at my age."

"It's just for tonight, Mum. Back to eating fruits and vegetables from tomorrow."

All three of us sit on the sofa and watch some TV while eating our food. It's the same sofa where I was sitting when Isabella appeared. A part of me wants to think that that night was a dream and none of that happened. Hans and Betty are watching some kind of Scottish drama that I've never heard of before while I am lost deep in my thoughts. I am glad when it's time to switch off the TV and go to bed. I am tired, very, very tired. Hans requests me to stay tonight as well and I oblige. I don't want to be alone right now in my house with my mother. I lie next to Hans for a few moments but when I can't make myself fall asleep, I find myself in the living room again sitting on the sofa.

"You look worried." I turn around and see Betty nervously standing there. She comes around the sofa and sits next to me. "Tell me, what's bothering you?" she asks.

"I am fine, Betty," I lie because I don't want to talk about Isabella. She's just going to deny everything.

"You're worried about Isabella," she says out of the blue.

I look up surprised. "Why did you pretend the other day that you don't know anything about Isabella? You are a part of her coven."

"Yes, I am. But I didn't want to say anything in front of Hans. I don't want him to find out that his mother is a witch and not a good Catholic woman as she pretends to be."

"He is not here right now. You can tell me everything. I am in trouble, Betty. Isabella is desperate for me to join her coven and I don't want to."

She nods and then holds my hand. Her hand is warm and as soon as she touches me, I know that she means no harm. Isabella may have ulterior evil motives but Betty doesn't. The way she looks at me, I can tell that she is innocent and just wants to help me. She starts to talk. "She wants you at any cost. This is why she attacked me. It was her way of punishing me. Because I didn't do my job properly."

"Punishing you? For what? What job?"

She takes a deep breath and leans against the sofa. She stares at the ceiling as she talks. "Do you remember the day you and I met, Kali?"

"Yeah, you almost killed me with your car." That day feels so long ago now. That day when Olive was new in my life and I had just got a job. I was so happy.

I hear Betty sighing. "Me meeting you wasn't a coincidence. It was orchestrated. I was given the task of testing you and then luring you to join our coven. But I guess I failed. I know this was before you even set Isabella free but it was written in your destiny. Even before you proved that you are worthy of joining our coven, we knew there was something special about you." I stay silent waiting for her to continue. "Kali, I don't want you to join our coven. Isabella doesn't want you to join us because she thinks you are some kind of powerful witch but because she wants to kill you and take away your magic."

"What? I have no magic, Betty." I huff. Isabella thinks I am strong and Betty thinks I have magic. They all believe I am someone special but I am not. I am just a girl trying to make the most of her circumstances.

"You do, Kali. You just don't know about them. As soon as you accept Isabella's invitation to join us, she will kill you. All of this is a trap. She can't hurt you right now because as I said, you are divinely protected, but once you join the coven, you'll transform. You won't be safe anymore. She is desperate because she is growing weaker. She was locked in that hut for years. Witches started questioning her, we all thought she wasn't a good leader for us if a priest could lock her away like that. None of us likes her. We want a new leader, a good one. None of us likes to do black magic but we have to follow her orders. Not all of us are murderers and kidnappers, Kali. We are good witches. We are just stuck with her."

"Can't you just kick her out from the coven if you don't like her?" I ask. All this magic and coven stuff is still new to me so I am not sure if my question is a stupid one or not. Nonetheless, Betty doesn't think I have a stupid question.

"No, we can't. It's much more complex than that. Besides, she rules us like she is a despot. Anyone who doesn't follow her orders has to pay. Numerous times she has hurt me and even hurts Hans sometimes just to get back at me. This is one of the reasons why I don't want you to join us. It is clear that Hans is in love with you and you are in love with him too. If you die, I don't think he'd be able to live without you."

Her words make me blush. With all that has been happening in my life, I haven't paid attention to Hans as much as I should have. Betty is right, we both have something strong. I don't know if it's love yet but I'd like to stay alive to find out. And I can't let Isabella come between us.

"Betty, you need to help me then. You need to show me how to win over her. I am new to everything so I don't know anything. But you must know a way."

"Kali, if I knew how, I would have done it myself," Betty says while massaging her forehead. All of this is stressful for her too.

We both stay silent for a moment. She is absolutely right. She cannot help me with this anymore, I have to do it myself now. I don't want to say it to her face but I can tell that she is not as strong a witch as Isabella. She doesn't stand a chance against Isabella's dark magic.

We are both silent for a moment, trying to think of something when I ask, "What's the deal with Berwick? Ruth asked me to search there."

"Ruth? How did you get in touch with her? She is dead, physically. Although she is just as much part of the coven as I am."

"I used an Ouija board. I know her granddaughter, Courtney."

"Oh. Wow. You've been doing magic already. So, Berwick is the place where a witch's initiation takes place. It's where a regular girl truly becomes a witch. It has been the seat of witches for hundreds of years. Perhaps you'll find something there that would help you win over Isabella."

I nod. I am intrigued to see what awaits me in Berwick.

"Kali?" Betty asks.

"Yeah?"

"Please take care of yourself. Not just Hans but even I have grown closer to you. I don't want any harm to befall you."

"I'll do my best, Betty. I'll do my best."

***

The next day I skip work again without telling Henry. I don't think I owe him anything anymore. If I want to take a day off, I will. And I won't seek his permission to do that. Instead, I write a long email to the History Department explaining the situation and asking for a meeting. I hope I get to hear something positive from them. After breakfast, Hans leaves for work and I leave for Berwick.

Before I am leaving, Betty comes to me and gives me her eye-pendant necklace. "This necklace will protect you." I already have it but I take Betty's necklace just in case.

"Thanks, Betty." She hugs me then and I melt. It's almost like having a parental figure hug me, it's something I am not used to experiencing. Perhaps when all of this is done, Betty can give me the motherly love I have always craved for.

I reach Berwick early in the morning but instead of heading straight to the castle, I look around. Something tells me there is more than what meets the eye. Not just the castle but something else must be the reason why a witch's initiation takes place in this town.

The first place I find myself is the museum. It's a tiny museum, not like the big museums in Glasgow or London. It's only a few rooms of paintings and artefacts. The receptionist is almost snoring when I ask to buy the ticket.

"It's free to enter but you have to leave your bag here." I do as she says.

The first room of the museum is covered with paintings on all the walls. I inspect each and every painting because my intuition tells me I'll find something here. And I do. In the corner of the room is a small painting of a man and his wife. The man is tall and handsome with a thin moustache. The wife is wearing a black dress and a white collar. It's Isabella. To my surprise, the painting doesn't refer to her as a witch or a criminal. The board under the painting doesn't mention her at all. Only the man's name is written. Richard Gowdie, a wealthy businessman who was a benefactor of the museum. There's a tiny slide with some information about Richard but nothing that would be of use to me. I find a woman standing in the corner who looks like she works for the museum. I go to her.

"Excuse me, can you tell me something about this man? The painting is beautiful."

"Oh, that's Mr Richard Gowdie, one of the wealthiest men in Scotland while he was alive. But alas he lost all of his wealth away in gambling. He died under mysterious circumstances, although most believe he died by suicide." I slowly nod my head. I highly doubt he committed suicide, it must have been Isabella who is responsible for his ruin.

"What about his wife? What kind of woman was she?" I ask feigning innocence on the topic.

She purses her lips. "She was a criminal and some locals even believe she was a witch. I have always believed that she brought bad luck to Richard's life. She was executed for her crime publicly although some believe that the priest imprisoned her in her hut. There are many rumours about her and it's hard to figure out what's true or not."

"Did she live here in Berwick?"

"Yeah, they both lived in Berwick while they were married. When he died, she moved away somewhere else. Perhaps Luss."

"Wow."

"Young lady, why are you so interested in learning about such dark people? There are many more figures in this room, much better figures."

"I have just always been interested in learning about dark history. You see, I work as a researcher for the University of Glasgow and I am doing a profile on witches. That's how I've come here. Can you tell me where they both lived in Berwick?"

"They lived in a house by the beach. It's about ten minutes away from Tantallon Castle. Although I would suggest you shouldn't go there."

"Why?" I ask.

"People believe it's haunted," she says without a smile on her face. I have no reason to believe she is wrong about it.

"Don't worry, Kayla," I read the name on her nametag. "I am not afraid of ghosts."

***

I walk to the house Kayla pointed out and it doesn't look scary at all. It looks like any other house to me. Sure, it looks a bit dirty from the outside and looks like it is in need of renovation but it doesn't seem haunted. I don't even know what a haunted house is supposed to look like. Without hesitation, I go inside and I am surprised at how clean it is from the inside, unlike its exterior. It doesn't look abandoned at all. It clearly means someone has been living here and who else could it be except Isabella?

But this house tells me much more than what I found in Isabella's hut. The walls are painted a bright shade of yellow and there are several stacks of bookcases. She loves to read. I inspect the different rooms and I almost scream when I hear something moving behind me. I suspect it's Isabella who is going to hurt me but I am surprised to see a black cat sitting on the floor purring. Olive!

I run to her and lift her up in my arms. "Oh, Olive. I missed you so much." Unlike other times, Olive doesn't try to wriggle out of my arms. In fact, she hugs me back, licking my ear. "You missed me too, didn't you?" I am glad to get my cat back. I know Olive works for Isabella but she was my cat once, she was the only creature who loved me back and I can't bring myself to hate her. Olive gives me another reason why I have to be free from Isabella's shackles.

She jumps out of my arms and looks at me as if she wants to show me something. She wants me to follow her. I walk behind her and she takes me to a small room on the top floor. The first thing I notice is that this room's a library. There is a desk in the centre with big bookshelves surrounding all the walls. Olive walks to the bookshelf and scratches one of the books.

I take the book and open it. It's a handwritten diary of someone. It doesn't mention whose it is but there is almost everything I need to know written on it. It's another copy of the book I found in the archives, the book that teaches girls how to become a witch. I take the book with me because I don't want to risk being found here in this house. I take the book and start walking and I am surprised to see Olive walking behind me.

"You want to come with me?" I can't help but smile. She may be forced to work for Isabella but she truly belongs to me. I pick her up in my arms and walk outside.

It's a sunny day outside and since it's an important book, I need to find a comfortable place to read it. I walk back to the cafe by the train station and unlike the last time I was here, it's open.

"Can I bring my cat inside?" I ask the barista.

She looks at me and then at Olive. "What a cute kitty. Of course, you can bring her."

I order myself a cup of coffee along with a bagel and start reading. It takes me the entire day to finish reading the book. I leave the cafe in the evening when it's dark outside but I no longer feel scared. I know what to do now.

I don't go inside the castle, there's no point in going there tonight since it's not a full moon. If I truly want to defeat Isabella, I must have patience or I might end up ruining everything. But before I take the train back to Glasgow, I write my name on the wall myself with a piece of chalk I surprisingly had in my bag. My name is the thirteenth name and thereby I have accepted a place in Isabella's coven. I know this makes me more vulnerable to Isabella but I know she won't attack me. She is waiting for a full moon night too.

I am a witch now and I am ready to face whatever is ahead of me.

I take Olive in my hands and bring her back to Glasgow. She's very quiet right now and hasn't stopped hugging me. I can tell that she's missed me too. By the time I am home, it's late.

"Where have you been, Kali?" my mother asks once I step inside my flat.

"I don't owe you an answer." I take off my coat and hang it behind the door. I really don't. I am not going to appease my mother anymore. I am not going to try to be nice to her when she doesn't do the same for me. Our relationship is over. It was over a long time ago and I am no longer going to beat a dead horse.

"You are my daughter, you owe me everything. And you've brought this dirty cat back?" she asks with her arms crossed. I turn around to look at her. I look like her a lot. It was something everyone used to tell me while I was growing up but I could never see it for myself. But now that I am looking at her, she looks a lot like me. It hurts to see my own face reflected on someone who is so vile towards me. I take a deep breath and briefly close my eyes.

"Look, Mom. You've overstayed your welcome. I think you should leave." I want her to leave. She didn't ask me before coming here. She should have. She knew that if she did, my answer would have been no. I was too weak to ask her to leave earlier but not anymore. Her presence is no longer welcome in my house. Ever since she's come, my mental health has been poor and I am apprehensive about spending time in my own house. Not anymore. This is my house and she can't stay here any longer.

My mother is understandably surprised. She may think I am a bad daughter but I have never treated her poorly. For the first time in my life, I am raising my voice against her. And she can't believe it. "What? Are you throwing your mother out of your house in the middle of the night?" She is exaggerating because it's not the middle of the night yet but she has a tendency to be overdramatic. Nonetheless, I don't want her to leave right now. I am not a monster.

"I am not asking you to leave right now but I'd really appreciate it if you leave as soon as possible. Tomorrow, if possible. You should call your boyfriend and ask him when he'll be here."

"I can't believe you are talking to me like that. I am your mother. I have every right to everything you own. I have every right to stay in this flat for as long as I like. I raised you, fed you, and sent you to school but I never made a fuss about it. You owe me everything."

"Oh, mother. You've always made a fuss about it, in fact, you are making a fuss right now. I moved all the way away from Birmingham to be away from you, you staying here with me isn't good for either of us. And yes you fed me and raised me because you chose to have a child. I didn't ask to be born. I didn't ask to be abused for so many years. Not anymore. As I said, you can stay here for as long as you have to but please leave as soon as you have made other arrangements."

"Kali." She walks towards me and tries to hug me but I push her away. "You can't manipulate me any longer. You can spend the night but by tomorrow, I expect you to be gone. Either call your boyfriend or book a hotel room. But you can't stay here." I don't wait for her to respond to this anymore and shut the door to my bedroom behind me. I was being nice to her to let her stay until she could find something else. But she doesn't even want to accept that.

I lie on my bed and a smile appears on my face. It feels good to call out my mother for what she has always put me through and finally seek freedom from her. Throughout my life, I kept hoping things would eventually be okay between my mother and me but they won't. They never will and I am no longer going to put up with her abuse.

I lie down on my bed feeling much lighter than I have felt in a while. Olive cuddles next to me and I just know that things will eventually be okay now. Soon I drift into sleep.

I wake up the next morning refreshed and ready to face the day. I pour Olive's food and water into her respective bowls and make myself a large breakfast of waffles dipped in maple syrup. I don't have to worry about eating too many sweets and gaining weight anymore, I have no one breathing down my neck all the time that I am fat. Being overweight wouldn't be the worst thing that could happen to me. And if things get out of control, I have magic to help me.

Olive and I eat our breakfast together when I hear my mother dragging her suitcase. I can't believe that she actually listened to me. I thought I'd wake to another argument but I think my mother has finally accepted that she can't push me around any longer.

"Kali, Greg is downstairs and he is coming to pick me up," she says.

"Bye," I say nonchalantly. I do realise that once my mother passes through the door, it will really be over for us. Our relationship, however poor it might be, will end. I feel a knot in my throat. She leaves her suitcase and walks into the kitchen. She looks at Olive and then at me.

"You are the most disgraceful daughter in the world and I wish I had aborted you while I was pregnant." It would be a lie if I say her words don't hurt but I try my best to not cry in front of her.

"Mother, the door is there." She looks at me for a moment and I brace myself for whatever vitriol she is going to spew at me but she says nothing. She drags all of her bags and shuts the door behind her with a loud bang.

It's over. It's really over. I will never have to put up with my mother's abuse ever again. There are tears on my cheeks and I am not sure if they are tears of happiness or sadness. I feel Olive brushing her head against my leg trying to comfort me.

"I am okay, Olive." And I realise that I really am okay. Maybe not completely but eventually I'll be. It's better to be alone than be with someone who doesn't respect me.

After breakfast, I take a shower and get dressed. I leave Olive alone and head to the History Department of the University of Glasgow. I go straight to the Dean's office and since I don't have an appointment, his assistant stops me.

"You need an appointment to meet him."

"No, I don't. It's urgent."

"Stop. Wait—" I leave her yelling and go inside. The Dean is surprised to see me. He lowers his glasses and asks, "I am sorry, I didn't know I have a meeting."

"No, sir. We didn't have a meeting. But I need to talk."

I take a seat at his table and tell him everything about Henry. I have already submitted a written application but it may not reach the right person at the right time. And I am tired of waiting, I want justice right now. Justice delayed is justice denied after all.

"These are serious allegations, Miss Kali. I must look into this as soon as possible."

"Yes. But I also want to tell you that I can't work with him under these circumstances and hence, I must resign."

"You shouldn't resign. We'll take action against him, you shouldn't have to quit this job."

"No, I should. I am sorry but it would be too disturbing for me to continue working here. I hope you understand." The Dean thinks for a moment and nods.

"I understand. But please know that you'll be duly compensated for your time. And I apologise once again for what happened to you."

The Dean tells me I will get a severance package and the Department will also begin an investigation as soon as possible. He speaks a lot of jargon but I am not sure if I believe any of it.

"I can assure you we will do our best to help you as much as we can," the Dean says. I don't believe any word of it. He's saying all of this to save his face but I am not worried about it. I have something else planned for Henry.

***

I go back home to Olive because I don't want to leave her alone anymore. Now that I have quit my job, I can spend more time with her.

I have quit my job because I just don't see myself working in an office anymore. I want to travel around Scotland, I want to go to the north in the Highlands and learn all the magic. Hopefully, I will find a better job, a job that suits my interests. I know money was an issue when I started this job but it's not anymore. I am not going to spend my precious time working on something I don't truly enjoy doing. I am young. I want to explore all my interests and options. I don't want to be immortal like Isabella but I want to live my life.

I think about how I didn't want to be a witch just a few days ago, I am still not sure if I really want to do this or not but I am willing to try. There's no other way of escaping Isabella.

"Olive, how do I call Isabella?" It's time I let Isabella know what I have decided but I do not know where I can find her.

Olive lifts her tail and walks inside my bathroom. I look in the mirror waiting for her to appear and she does in a few seconds.

"Have you made your decision?" she asks. She has a smile on her face which I know is deceptive.

"I want to join your coven, Isabella," I tell her.

"Oh, Kali. I knew you'd eventually say yes to me." She looks happy, so happy that I can see she almost doesn't believe that I have said yes.

"But I have a condition."

"A condition?" Her smile falters a little bit.

"I want to be the leader of the coven."

She laughs but when I don't, she asks, "Are you crazy? You don't even know how to be a witch and you want to lead us? That will not be possible."

"Oh, come on. You can teach me everything."

"Do you even know what being the leader of the coven would mean?"

"I actually don't know. Why don't you tell me?"

"Each coven has a purpose, we don't use magic for the sake of using magic. We want to help people and it's the leader who chooses who to help. It's not just some women's club, it's much more serious than that."

"I think I can make those choices."

"You don't understand, the leader is much stronger than other witches. You aren't strong."

"You said that I am stronger than you are."

"Yes, but that's different. You are good, innocent, too pure. You have to face your dark side to become the leader. You have to hurt people even when you don't want to."

"Is this why you killed your husband?"

"What? Who told you that I killed my husband?" She looks offended. She doesn't want to accept that she's a murderer.

"No one. But isn't it suspicious? A wealthy man found dead under mysterious circumstances. And not just your husband, you have killed more people, innocent girls who wanted nothing to do with you."

"That's part of being a witch. It may sound bad but that's the truth." She is fumbling for words.

"No, that's not what being a witch means. Witches use their magic to heal, not kill. No one in the coven except you has killed people."

"How did you find all of that?"

"Betty told me. You tried to hurt her too."

"I hurt her because I asked her to lure you into the coven and she couldn't do that. Of course, she had to be punished."

"And why did you put my mother under your spell?"

"What makes you think that she was under your spell? She hated you, of course, she tried to kill you."

"Isabella, that's what you don't understand. You are full of darkness inside you, you can't be the leader of the coven with so much malice within you. It's because of witches like you that the witches through the centuries have been burnt, innocent witches who were using their magic for the good."

"You don't understand, you silly girl. You can't become our leader." I can see her growing angry now. She didn't expect this at all. She was expecting me to be meek and docile and do whatever she says. I won't do that.

"Then I won't join your coven."

"You have to. You have already followed all the steps, you've worn the necklace, you've adopted the black cat and you wrote your name on the wall. You are one of us now. You have no other option left. Come join us, Kali. When I die, you can become the leader."

Isabella is cunning. She knows how to play this game. Although I have learnt that if I truly want to win, I have to let her think that she's winning for now.

"Alright, Isabella. I will join you. I will join your coven."

She smiles at me. "Meet us outside the Tantallon Castle on the night of the full moon. We'll initiate you in our coven."

Chapter 9

On the night of the full moon, I find myself outside the castle. The wait for the full moon was excruciating but I am here now. But I didn't come alone. Courtney came with me to Berwick but she's at the cafe. I didn't expect her to come so close to me but she and I have become really good friends. She knows much more about witchcraft than I do. I am willing to learn now without any judgements.

As I walk to the castle, I see twelve women standing in a circle on the beach with candles in their hands. They are all wearing black dresses along with white collars. According to the book I read, some witches believe their magic is more potent when they wear black and white. To match them, I am wearing a similar dress. I am one of them now, I might as well dress like them.

Betty is the first one to spot me, she waves at me. Isabella, who is standing in the middle of the circle, looks at me. "Welcome, Kali."

Under the moonlight, her dead, pale skin looks even more disgusting. Isabella directs me to stand in the middle of the circle.

"For you to be initiated in our coven, all the witches must respond with a 'yes.'" She turns to all the witches, "You must all respond whether you accept Kali as one of us now or not."

Women in the circle one by one respond with a 'yes'. I know it's only for a show, they all have to do whatever Isabella asks them to do. When the last one of them has said yes, Isabella says, "Now, Kali. You are one of us now. You are truly a part of our coven."

I don't feel any different from how I was feeling moments ago. I feel exactly the same. They all begin to chant loudly while I stand there confused. "We are the witches you did burn, over and over again. And now we are back to reclaim our innate power. To burn away the toxic injustice that's become a disease on our beautiful mother Gaia. We embrace our Lilith energy."

Isabella turns to me, "Now let's help you cast your first spell. As you know we work against human monsters, men who have tormented women. Do you have any suggestions?"

"Henry, my boss. He harassed me." I don't even have to think about it. I was waiting for this moment I'd actually get to punish Henry.

One of the witches turns around and comes back with a bowl of clay. "Make an effigy of Henry as best as you can."

I was never good with art so making a small Henry out of clay isn't very easy. I make a little man out of clay as best as I can. It doesn't look much like Henry when it's done but Isabella tells me it will do the job.

"Now you must burn Henry's effigy in the fire or whatever else you want to do with it." I look at Henry's clay self in my hand. Yes, Henry hurt me but do I want to kill him? No. What would be the difference between him and me then? He harassed me but it doesn't mean that he deserves death for it. The crime should be commensurate with the punishment. Burning him in the fire wouldn't be justice for him harassing me. If I kill him, I'll also end up hurting his family, friends and people who love him. They don't deserve that pain.

"I don't want to do this, Isabella," I tell her out loud. I hear a few gasps from the circle around me. Perhaps they didn't expect the new witch to tell Isabella no.

"What do you mean?" Isabella is confused too. I can tell she's not used to hearing no.

"I don't want to kill him," I repeat.

All the witches look at each other, just as confused as I am.

"But this is your first ritual. You can't leave it incomplete," Isabella says.

"I am not going to leave it incomplete. Don't worry. I will do something else."

"What are you going to do?"

"I want to hurt Henry, not physically. I don't want to kill him. I just want him to be in emotional pain, I want him to feel remorse for what he did and never do it to another woman again. I want the rest of the girls to believe me and see the truth for what it is."

"Kali, you are weak. We must kill him, we must kill all men. We must kill anyone who hurts us. That is the only way of seeking justice." Isabella is fuming and she's almost shouting now.

I have been a part of the coven only for a few minutes and I am already fighting with Isabella.

"Isabella, do I have to do everything you tell me to do? Is that what being a part of this coven means?"

She stares at me and then smiles. "Of course, not. Killing someone can be daunting when you're new. I understand that. Perhaps we should do some other spell to initiate you in our coven. Do you want to learn how to make a potion that makes you never grow old?"

"Yeah, that's something I'd like."

"Good. Let's go inside the castle."

As we all walk inside the castle, I feel a hand on my waist. It's Betty. "What are you doing?"

"I am going inside."

"Yes, but denying what Isabella asks you to do is a death sentence. You should have just burnt Henry's effigy in the fire."

"I don't want to do that, Betty. That's barbaric."

"That's what being a witch in Isabella's coven is. We have to hurt people who give us trouble. Things weren't like this when she was still trapped but now she's free."

"I am not going to kill anybody, Betty."

"Lass, you must stay vigilant. You are digging your own grave." She drops her hand and walks in front of me.

Inside the castle, I am given a cauldron and a few ingredients to make the potion. Thanks to the book I read in Isabella's library, I know how to do this very well. How strong your potion is depends on the strength of the witch who is making it. And I know I am strong. I can tell Isabella is upset with me that I am doing this rather than murdering someone. When the moon is high in the sky and I am done making the potion, Isabella tells me, "We meet every full moon with a list of men we must get rid of to make this world a better place. We did not kill anyone tonight but next month, I won't be so lenient with you."

I nod. Isabella turns to other witches, "I hope all of you will help Kali become a part of us. She's new and doesn't know our ways. We must help her find direction."

"Isabella, will you try the potion that I have made? I don't know if it works or not." I hand her a cup of the potion that I've made.

"Sure."

She takes a sip and then looks at me admiringly. "It tastes like it might work. Good job."

A few seconds pass and the smile on her face disappears. "My insides are burning. Are you sure you put in all the right ingredients, Kali?"

"I did. But I have not made the potion that makes witches look young. I have made the potion that would kill you, Isabella. You wanted me to murder someone to be a part of this coven. And this is exactly what I did." I had read the book in Isabella's house well and I knew I was going to make this potion sooner than later. I collected all the ingredients with the help of Courtney and put them in a small bag.

Before Isabella can say anything, she's on fire. We back away just in case we don't catch it too. She burns like a huge pyre in front of us, screaming and drowning in flames.

"She's dead?" Betty asks when the fire has burnt out and there's nothing left on the ground.

"Yes. She will no longer haunt us."

"But now we are once again twelve, we'd need to find a new member," I hear someone say. I find it amusing that the first thing someone says after Isabella has died is that we need to find a new member to replace her.

"I have someone in mind. In fact, she's waiting for us at the cafe. We must initiate her before the sun comes out." I quickly call Courtney and ask her to walk to the castle. "It's time," I tell her.

As we wait for Courtney to walk to us, I realise that Isabella is gone, she is gone forever now. She won't haunt me again. I take Olive in my arms and kiss her on the head. Tonight, I'll sleep peacefully.

Epilogue

"I don't think I'll ever get enough of this view," Hans says to me and I couldn't agree more. We are looking down at everything around us as we are standing at the Old Man of Storr, a rocky hill that took us a while to climb.

We are sitting down in companionable silence.

"I am so glad we are finally here," I tell Hans as I hold his hand.

It's been a while since I have become a witch. My life has changed drastically but I don't think it's because I am a witch now. Something has changed deep within me and I am glad for it. So many toxic things are gone from my life.

My mother.

My job.

Isabella.

I have spent the past few months getting to know myself better. I didn't apply for a job but I started working as a tarot reader online. Since it's a new business, I am not rolling in cash but I earn enough to get by. Thanks to my witchy spells, all my predictions come true and my clients keep returning for more. Every morning I wake up, do a little bit of reading and then I get outside the house. I walk for hours and hours, sometimes within the city and sometimes I take the train and come to the Highlands. I read books and then write in my journal.

The real magic doesn't happen because of the spells I've learnt. The real magic happens because I am finally at peace with who I am. I am no longer doing what everyone expects me to do. I am doing what I think I should do. As a result, my relationships with other people are also getting better. Hans and I have got a lot closer. I am not rushing into anything because I know that only leads to disasters. I am taking it slow, getting to know him better so that when I am finally with him, I know I have made the right choice. My mother hasn't got in touch with me and neither have I. I know she'll try to talk to me though. She'd want to know what's going on in my life. I don't think I'd completely sever contact with my mother but I am also not going to initiate any contact. Olive continues to be my best friend. I am becoming a better mother to her every day.

I moved to Glasgow to change my life and I finally did, although in a different way than I had imagined it to be. I am very excited to see what lies ahead of me.

"Should we get some coffee now? It's freezing up here," Hans asks as he rubs his hands together.

"Yes, Hans. Let's get some coffee."

About the Author

Vidhipssa Mohan is the author of paranormal and urban fantasy novels. She wanted to live in a world with magic but since the real world is too dreary, she puts the magic in her books.

Subscribe to my newsletter to stay in touch.

Read more at https://mailchi.mp/c295eb2943de/vidhipssa.

Printed in Great Britain
by Amazon